WRONG TWIN
RIGHT BRIDE

PATRICIA KAY

Silhouette®

SPECIAL EDITION®

Published by Silhouette Books

America's Publisher of Contemporary Romance

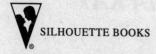

SILHOUETTE BOOKS

ISBN-13: 978-0-373-65531-1

Recycling programs
for this product may
not exist in your area.

WRONG GROOM, RIGHT BRIDE

Visit Silhouette Books at www.eHarlequin.com

Printed in U.S.A.

PATRICIA KAY

Formerly writing as Trisha Alexander, Patricia Kay is a *USA TODAY* bestselling author of more than forty-eight novels of contemporary romance and women's fiction. She lives in Houston, Texas. To learn more about her, visit her Web site at www.patriciakay.com.

This book is dedicated to Pat Rosen—for all those wonderful reviews, but especially for being my friend.

Chapter One

Chloe Patterson couldn't stop smiling as she put the finishing touches on her makeup. She kept thinking she should pinch herself, make sure everything that had happened to her in the past six months wasn't a dream. First her engagement to Todd Hopewell, one of the most sought-after bachelors in Riverton, New York, then the incredible news she had confirmed only this week.

But neither was a dream. The magnificent two-carat sparkler on the ring finger of her left hand was certainly very real. Moving her hand closer to the rays of late afternoon sunlight streaming through her bedroom window, she watched, mesmerized, as the jewel-like colors burst into the air.

Oh, she was so excited and happy! Life was going so well, so incredibly well. There was so much to look forward to. From now on, there would only be light in her life. The dark days were all in the distant past, and they could no longer affect her.

Shivering with anticipation at the thought of seeing her fiancé again, she spritzed herself with the light fragrance she favored, then rummaged in her jewelry box for her favorite gold hoop earrings.

Almost a month was too long for her and Todd to be apart, she thought yet again, especially when their wedding day was less than six weeks away. She knew he must feel the same way. Just because he'd seemed a little distant lately and hadn't called or texted much since he'd been in California didn't mean a thing.

He wasn't neglecting her. It was just that he was so busy. She knew how important the assignment in San Francisco was to him. To them and their future. He'd explained that he needed to prove something to his family—that this was the first time he'd been entrusted with an existing project and potential future business this important to the company. That the harder he worked, the sooner he could come home. And now…in just a few short minutes he would be there.

Back to me.

Back to us.

Gently, she touched her stomach—still flat, still concealing her delicious secret. Of course, she was only about a month along—she figured she'd conceived the night before Todd left for the coast—and it was way too soon to be showing. In fact, she hadn't even seen a doctor yet, but she'd used two pregnancy tests. And both were positive.

Besides, her breasts were tender, and she'd even felt a bit nauseous once or twice. She was definitely pregnant. For the past couple of days—ever since she'd confirmed to herself that she was going to have a baby—she'd almost been afraid to be *too* happy. It was hard not to, though. She'd wanted a baby since she was old enough to think about such things. She still found it hard to believe that all her dreams would soon come true—that she'd have a husband and a child—a family and a home all her own.

Would Todd be as happy about the baby as she was? She hoped he wouldn't think it was too soon. After all, she was almost thirty, and he was thirty-two. They were hardly children. Surely he would be happy.

Biting her lip, she wondered what his mother would say when she realized Chloe was pregnant. At the thought of the coolly elegant Larissa Lenore Hopewell and that assessing way she had of looking at Chloe as if she didn't quite measure up to the Hopewell standards, some of Chloe's happiness faded.

What was it about Todd's mother that was so intimidating? Why was it that Chloe, who was so confident in her professional life, who had been independent and pretty much self-supporting since she was eighteen, could be reduced to a babbling idiot by one of Larissa's just-short-of-openly-critical comments?

"Oh, stop thinking about her," she muttered to herself. Still, she couldn't help but remember how Todd had never once contradicted her when she said she didn't think his mother liked her. Then again, Todd never contradicted *anything* his mother said, did he?

Chloe pushed aside the disloyal thought. Of course he was solicitous of his mother and her opinions. They were important to him and his future—*their* future—which was so closely aligned with his family. Things would be different when they were married. She would just have to be patient with him, that's all.

Still, it was important what Larissa Hopewell thought. Every woman wanted her future mother-in-law to approve of her. After all, Todd's mother would be their child's grandmother—the only grandmother he or she would have, since Chloe's mother was long gone. Most important, this baby would be the *first* Hopewell grandchild because neither of Todd's two older brothers had children yet. Surely...*surely* that would be important to Larissa.

Chloe sighed. She would just have to work harder to win Todd's mother over. The thought had barely formed when the doorbell rang.

Chloe's heart skidded. *Todd!*

Rushing from the bedroom, she hurried down the stairs and across the entryway. She nearly tripped on the stack of boxes leaning against the wall—boxes she'd been meaning to begin using to pack up her belongings for the move to Todd's place. "Todd!" she cried, flinging open the front door of the rented townhome.

But it wasn't Todd.

Instead, a FedEx driver stood on the doorstep. "Ms. Patterson?"

"Yes."

"Delivery for you. Sign here, please."

She eyed the overnight envelope as she signed the delivery ticket.

"Thanks." He smiled briefly, handed her the envelope and then walked rapidly back to his truck.

Frowning, Chloe closed the door slowly. The return address on the label said the envelope had come from Todd—sent from San Francisco. What in the world? Had she gotten the dates wrong? Had something happened? Was he not coming home today?

With mounting trepidation, she pulled the strip that opened the package. Inside there was one lone sheet of paper. Even before she pulled it out, her heart began knocking against her chest.

Dear Chloe,
I know this will be a shock. Yesterday Meredith and I were married. When you get this, we will be on our honeymoon in Fiji. We fought our feelings for each other for weeks now, but it was no use. I hope someday you'll forgive me. The ring is yours. Sell it if you want. I'm sorry.
Todd

Shocked and disbelieving, Chloe stared at the paper as if staring long and hard enough would change the words to something that made sense.

Married! To Meredith!

She shook her head. No. This couldn't be happening. Meredith Belson was Todd's assistant. A childhood friend of his. She…she had been so nice to Chloe. She'd even recommended a wedding planner to help Chloe with all the details for her upcoming wedding. She had believed Meredith to be her friend, too. In fact, aside from Molly, Chloe's cousin and best friend, Meredith was the *last* person Chloe would ever have imagined would betray her like this.

Shaking, Chloe walked to the stairs and sat down. Samson, her cat, sensing her distress, sidled up to her and meowed.

Chloe kept staring at the stark words. *Yesterday Meredith and I were married.*

How could she?

But it's not Meredith's fault, is it? She's not the one who said he loved you. She's not the one who asked you to marry him. Todd is the one who betrayed you.

Chloe was too numb, still too shocked to cry. Todd. Todd and all the bright dreams of the future he had brought into her life…were gone.

Married.

To someone else.

Keep the ring. Sell it if you want.

As those cruel words echoed, tears finally filled Chloe's eyes, but these weren't sad tears. They were angry tears. Wrenching the ring off her finger, she threw it against the wall. Samson jumped in alarm and, in a blur of ocher fur, raced away.

The flawless stone set in platinum fell to the floor. It lay there, a glittering, forlorn symbol of what would never be.

What am I going to do?

And it was only then that the most serious consequence of Todd's betrayal really hit her.

Our baby.

Oh, God. How could she have forgotten the baby? The baby Todd didn't know about.

She swallowed hard, clutching her stomach. A wild hope flooded her. Surely, when Todd *did* know, he would realize he'd made a terrible mistake. He would come back to her. To *them.* She had to tell him. Right now. Even though he'd said he and Meredith were on their honeymoon in Fiji, Chloe knew Todd well enough to know he would never be without his BlackBerry.

I'll text him.

Yet even as she started up the stairs to find her cell phone, she knew texting Todd was a crazy idea. Did she want Todd back because he felt guilty? Of course she didn't. She wanted him to love her! She wanted him to *want* to be with her. No way was she going to try to blackmail him or guilt him into anything.

Once more, she sank down onto one of the steps. This time the tears that ran down her face were filled with heartbreak.

She would have her baby alone.

In fact, she didn't want Todd to *ever* know about their baby. If he had rejected them, they would reject him.

No matter what it cost her.

Simon Foster Hopewell III had the beginnings of a monster headache as he reviewed the revised budget for the fiscal year beginning next month on the first of June.

He couldn't believe what a botched mess this latest version of the production department budget was. And this was the *third* time it had been revised. Picking up a red felt-tip pen he angrily crossed out items one by one. Somehow his department heads needed to understand that they had to stay within the guidelines they'd been given, whether they liked it or not. Maybe they operated like this at home, borrowing from Peter to pay Paul, but they were not going to operate like this at Hopewell Enterprises. Not as long as he was in charge.

Blowing out an exasperated breath, Simon sat back in his swivel chair and glanced up at the large oil portrait of his great grandfather, the first Simon Hopewell, for whom he'd been named. A stern man who came from Quaker stock, he'd be appalled at the way business was conducted nowadays. Old Simon had never borrowed a penny in his life.

Simon closed his eyes. He was tired. Tired of being the heavy here at the company and tired of being the heavy at home. Ever since his father had died two years ago of a sudden, massive heart attack, most of the responsibility for both the business and the family had fallen onto his shoulders.

Certainly he got no help from Noah, who wanted nothing to do with the business and spent his days working at a homeless shelter and his nights fooling around with the rock band he'd started. Noah was a good guy; Simon actually admired him for his convictions and his lack of interest in money, but he had to face facts. Noah was never going to play a part in the Hopewell family fortunes.

And the jury was still out on Todd. If he did a good job with the clients in San Francisco, then Simon might consider giving him more responsibility within the business. But Simon wasn't convinced that would happen. In fact, he'd been worrying ever since he'd entrusted Todd with the San Francisco assignment.

Todd was spoiled. He was also impulsive, always jumping into things. He started out enthusiastic, but his interest could quickly wane. He had been indulged by their mother from the day he was old enough to understand he was her favorite. He really didn't like to work hard, although he could talk a good game and was so charming he fooled a lot of people into thinking there was substance there.

One thing Todd *had* done right, though, was choose wisely when it came to the woman he planned to marry. His choice had surprised Simon, especially after hearing what his mother had to say about Todd's fiancée, but after meeting Chloe Patterson, Simon had decided his mother was wrong. Simon liked Chloe. From the beginning, she'd struck him as sensible and practical, the kind of woman who would temper Todd's tendencies to plunge without thinking.

And after investigating her privately—Simon hadn't wanted to, but he'd known if he didn't, his mother would, and he'd decided him doing the deed was the lesser of two evils—he'd been even more reassured. Yes, Chloe was literally from the wrong side of Riverton's tracks. Yes, her mother had deserted Chloe and her father when Chloe was only eight years old—left them for a much younger lover and come to a bad end five years later, and yes, her father had become an alcoholic and committed suicide a couple of years later. Also, Chloe hadn't gone to an Ivy League school the way the Hopewell brothers had, and she would bring no money or position to the marriage.

But—and Simon considered these attributes more important than money or position or anything else—she had gone to work at eighteen, educated herself by taking some night courses at the local community college and started her own Web design business while holding down a full-time job at a small tech company in nearby Mohawk. According to the investigator, she had grossed more than sixty-five thousand dollars from the business last year and was on track to do better this year. She had health insurance and owned a paid-for car, and she had a decent savings account—not riches, certainly—but enough so that if she'd wanted to buy her own condo or small house, she could've managed a down payment.

She was a strong young woman, and she would be good for Todd. Simon was certain of that.

And she was lovely, with a charming smile, beautiful green eyes and thick, shiny brown hair. A girl-next-door type. Just the kind of woman Simon liked best. She also had long, gorgeous legs. And Simon was definitely a leg man.

Too bad I didn't meet her first.

It wasn't the first time Simon had thought this. But you had to make an effort if you wanted to meet the kind of woman who would make a great wife and mother, and Simon hadn't made any kind of effort at all since his love affair with Alexis had gone south.

Just then his intercom buzzed, and thoughts of Alexis and Chloe and Todd disappeared as he picked up the phone.

"Your brother's on the line," Maggie, his secretary, said.

"Noah?"

"Todd."

Simon glanced at the Wedgwood clock sitting on his antique mahogany desk. Todd must be back. "Welcome home," he said when Maggie connected them. "How was your flight?"

"Uh, listen, Simon, I'm, uh, not home. I'm, uh, calling from Fiji."

"Fiji! What the…what are you doing *there?*"

Simon listened thunderstruck as Todd explained. His heart beat ominously, and the headache that had begun earlier erupted full force. He knew if Todd had been there in the room with him, he would have had a hard time restraining himself from strangling the little worm.

"You bastard," he said when Todd fell silent. "How could you do something so irresponsible and cowardly?"

As Todd sputtered and tried to justify himself, saying things like "I couldn't help it" and "I've always loved Meredith" and "Chloe was a big mistake, even Mom thought so!" Simon got angrier and angrier.

"Does Chloe know?" he ground out.

"I, uh, sent her a letter."

"You sent her a letter," Simon repeated flatly.

"Yeah, I, uh, thought it was…the best way."

"You are even more of a horse's ass than I thought."

"That's not fair, Simon! Christ, you act like I killed somebody. I just broke an engagement."

"No, you didn't *just* break an engagement. You betrayed and humiliated a good person, someone who didn't deserve to be treated that way. And, as usual, you expect someone else to clean up your mess."

"What mess? You don't have to do anything. Stop treating me like I'm a child."

"Then quit acting like one. When are you coming home? When am I going to get a full report on San Francisco?"

"You'll have your report tomorrow," Todd said, his voice filled with resentment. "I'll fax it to you. And Meredith and I aren't coming home till next week. Maybe not then, either. We deserve a nice honeymoon."

This final justification for his bad behavior filled Simon with disgust, but he was sick of talking to his brother, so instead of answering, he simply hung up on him.

"Did Todd call you?" Simon asked his mother. Instead of phoning her after his conversation with Todd, Simon had told Maggie he was leaving for the day and to cancel his production department meeting that afternoon. "Tell them I'll see them in the morning." Then he'd driven to the family home in Riverton's beautiful Maple Hill district.

"Yes, he did," Larissa Hopewell said. Her pleased expression spoke volumes.

"And you're not upset?"

"Well, I certainly would have preferred he never got engaged to her in the first place. You know I never approved of his involvement with that woman from the beginning."

That woman. She can't even say her name. Simon chose his words carefully. "But his wedding to Chloe was supposed to take place in less than six weeks. The church, the country club, everything is already booked. Don't you think what he did was not only unkind to her but immature and thoughtless, that it doesn't reflect well on our family's name?" *The family name you feel is so damned important?*

"Honestly, Simon, sometimes I don't understand you," his mother retorted, blue eyes glittering with indignation. "Where's your loyalty? You should be glad he dumped her. She would never have fit into our family, and you know it. Why, she wasn't *worthy* of having our family's name."

"I know no such thing," Simon said coldly. "I liked her. I thought she would have been good for Todd." *And a breath of fresh air for us.*

"I don't know how you can say that. She's common. Simply not in our class. I doubt their marriage would have lasted a year."

Simon gritted his teeth to keep from saying what he was thinking. What good would it do? His mother would never change. "And you don't think we owe her something? At the very least I think we should pay whatever out-of-pocket expenses she incurred in the planning of the wedding."

His mother shrugged her narrow, elegant shoulders. "Fine. Go ahead. Make the offer."

"So you agree?"

"Whether I agree or not is irrelevant, isn't it? You

always do just as you please, anyway. As do your brothers. Even Todd. But at least he's finally come to his senses and recognized that when it comes to *that woman* I was right all along."

And with that, she turned back to the invitation she'd been answering when he'd interrupted her by his visit.

Simon stared at her blue silk-clad back for one long moment before saying, "Goodbye, Mother." He lingered a couple of seconds, but she didn't turn around.

As he walked out to his car, he decided he would not wait another day before calling on Chloe and offering his help.

He only hoped she would see him.

Because, in her shoes, he might slam the door in the face of any Hopewell who dared to cross her doorstep.

Chapter Two

Chloe couldn't sleep. Finally, at about three o'clock in the morning, she gave up, much to Samson's consternation. Her cat—who spent his nights at the foot of her bed—wasn't used to a change in routine. But he rallied and followed her downstairs and into the kitchen, where she put the kettle on. She would have a cup of hot chocolate and try to figure out what she was going to do now that her future had been torpedoed.

Samson figured if she was going to be up and about that it must be time for her to feed him, so he pestered her until she put food in his bowl. She couldn't help chuckling as she watched him happily chowing down. What would she do without his company? Hopefully, she wouldn't have to find out.

Carrying her mug and a sleeve of Ritz crackers into the living room, she curled up into her favorite chair. Although she hadn't turned on a lamp, moonlight streamed through the big window that overlooked the quiet street and illuminated the room. Normally, when she went to bed at night, she pulled the drapes closed, but last night and again tonight—ever since that letter from Todd arrived—she hadn't been herself.

What am I going to do?

If she wasn't pregnant, she wouldn't have a dilemma. She'd still be upset over the way Todd had treated her, yes, and there might have been some embarrassing moments when the two of them ran into each other— as inevitably would have happened in a town the size of Riverton—but she could have handled all that.

Only she was pregnant.

As she'd done so often recently, she touched her stomach.

"I want you," she whispered. "No matter what, I want you."

Chloe wondered what her aunt Jane and cousin Molly would think when they found out about the broken engagement and the pregnancy. She had almost called them yesterday but decided she wanted to have a better idea of what she was going to do before she told them what had happened. Not calling the two people who'd been her only family for a long time was one of the hardest things she'd ever had to do, but she wanted to be sure she wouldn't break down when they talked. She didn't want them worrying about her. This was *her* problem, not theirs.

The sky was showing its first blush in the east when she arrived at the reluctant conclusion that she wouldn't be able to remain in Riverton. Not if she wanted to keep her baby away from the Hopewell family. Riverton was too small a town. If she continued to live there, the Hopewells were bound to find out about the baby, and then who knew what would happen? They might try to discredit her in some way or, worse, try to take the baby away from her.

No. She absolutely couldn't risk it, no matter how much it hurt to think about leaving her aunt and cousin. There was no alternative but to move. Thank goodness she could work anywhere. As the owner of her own Web design and marketing business, all she required to service her clients was her computer and a telephone.

Sighing, she got up and headed into her office. After settling down at her desk, she pulled out her ledger, logged on to the Internet and accessed her bank account.

For the next hour, she did some calculating. When she was finished, it was clear that if she did what Todd had so coldly suggested and sold her engagement ring she ought to have enough money to cover a move from Riverton, as well as the expenses she'd incur by having the baby on her own. It would be close, but she'd be able to manage without touching her savings. She heaved a sigh. She wished she had the luxury of throwing the ring in Todd's face. But she had to be practical. Pride was important, yes, but the well-being of her child was even more important. So her pride would suffer a little. So what?

She wondered how long she had before she started showing. So far nothing about her body looked different. Maybe her breasts were slightly swollen but not noticeably. She did some mental calculation. It was the middle of May. She figured for at least another month or so, she would be okay, especially if she wore tops a little roomier than usual. But she imagined by the middle of July or certainly by the first of August, she'd no longer be able to hide her pregnancy. So she would need to move fairly soon—probably by the first of July. Which meant she had about six weeks to make all her arrangements. Since she'd already been planning to move from her townhouse to Todd's place after the wedding, at least her landlord already had his notice. Now that she'd made some decisions about her future, she felt better.

After taking a quick shower and getting dressed, she figured it was late enough to call at her aunt's without waking them up.

"'Morning, Chloe," her aunt said.

Chloe could hear the smile in her aunt's voice. "Hi, Aunt Jane. I didn't wake you, did I?"

"Of course not. I've been up since six, and Molly just got out of the shower. Did you want to talk to her?"

"No, actually I thought I might pop over to talk to both of you. That is, if you don't have plans."

"No, no plans. I might work in the garden later and, as you know, Molly always has a ton of errands on Saturdays, but both of those things can wait. You're always welcome. Is…there anything wrong?" Now her voice was laced with concern.

"No, not exactly wrong. I just, um…I'll tell you when I get there, okay?

"Okay, honey. I'll put a fresh pot of coffee on. Have you had breakfast yet?"

Chloe smiled. "Do a few crackers in the middle of the night count?"

Thirty minutes later, Chloe pulled up and parked in front of the small bungalow in one of the oldest sections of Riverton, where her aunt had lived ever since Chloe could remember. Everywhere she looked were good memories. The huge maple tree that sheltered the left side of the house had held a tire swing that Molly and Chloe loved, and its strong branches were just made for climbing. They'd roller-skated on the sidewalks and had tea parties with their dolls on the wide front porch. Sadly, she thought how much she would miss coming here as often as she did now. But it couldn't be helped.

When her petite aunt—looking almost as young as her daughter, dressed as she was in cropped denim pants and a bright red T-shirt—opened the front door, her welcoming smile warmed Chloe. Jane's brown eyes reflected her trepidation, though, and Chloe knew her aunt was worried by her uncharacteristic request to come over this morning. Normally Chloe would just drop in without calling. The fact she'd asked had sent a signal.

They hugged, and Jane said, "Molly's in the kitchen. And there are corn muffins in the oven and bacon in the microwave."

Chloe smiled. "My favorites."

"I know."

Suddenly, Chloe's eyes filled with tears. Her aunt, who never missed anything, saw them.

"Oh, hon, what is it?" She put her arm around Chloe's shoulders and squeezed.

Chloe shook her head, upset with herself for getting emotional. She'd promised herself she wouldn't, that she'd simply tell Jane and Molly the facts about what had happened and then talk practicalities. The last thing she wanted was to upset them.

Molly, hands encased in oven mitts, was sliding a muffin tin out of the oven as they walked into the sunny kitchen. The smile on her face faded as she saw Chloe's expression. Putting the tin down on the stove, she walked over and enfolded Chloe in a hug. "Is it Todd?" she asked.

Chloe nodded, then managed to get a grip. Sighing heavily, she extricated herself from Molly's embrace and sank onto a kitchen chair. The smell of the cooked bacon permeated the kitchen. Molly took off the oven mitts, tossed them onto a counter and took a chair opposite her. "Tell us," she demanded.

"The engagement is off," Chloe said.

"Oh, Chloe," her aunt said. She was already pouring a mug of coffee, which she handed to Chloe.

"What happened?" Molly asked. Her brown eyes, the exact shade of her mother's, were filled with worry.

Chloe grimaced. "What happened? He married Meredith. Even now they are on their honeymoon. In Fiji."

Molly's mouth dropped open, and Jane gasped. "Married!" they both exclaimed at once.

"What a dirtbag!" Molly said. "How did you find out?"

"He sent me a letter. Via FedEx."

"Via *FedEx!*" If anything, Molly's voice had risen an octave. Her eyes now flashed fire and outrage.

Jane shook her head. "I am so sorry, honey. That must have hurt."

"You could say that."

"Are you okay?"

"I'm going to be. I'm determined to be, actually. I don't think Todd is worth wasting too many tears on."

"You can say *that* again," Molly said indignantly. "I never did like him."

Chloe couldn't help it. She laughed. "You did so."

"No, I didn't. He's altogether too good-looking and too sure of himself. I don't trust men who have everything. They always think they're somehow entitled. He seemed…I don't know…weak, the way he never stood up to that mother of his. And you said yourself that he'd had some problems finding himself." She rolled her eyes. "*Finding* himself. That's a good one."

"You never said anything."

Molly shrugged. "You were so happy. I hoped I was wrong."

"I wasn't crazy about him, either," Jane said quietly.

"You *weren't?*" Chloe was shocked by this admission. She'd believed that her aunt and her cousin were thrilled with the match she'd made. In fact—and it shamed her to admit it, even to herself—she'd thought Molly was probably secretly envious.

"He's just a little too slick for my taste," Jane said. "But I, too, hoped I was wrong."

"We talked about it," Molly confessed. "Whether we should tell you about our reservations."

"I wish you had," Chloe said bitterly.

"Would you have listened?" Jane asked.

Chloe sighed. "Probably not."

"Chloe…" Molly hesitated. "Why *did* you get engaged to Todd? I never could figure it out. I mean, to me, you were a mismatch from the beginning."

"I don't know," Chloe admitted. "I think I was flattered. Plus—" and this was hard to admit, even to these two, whom she loved more than anyone "—I think I wanted a family of my own so badly that I allowed that to color my judgment where Todd was concerned."

"Oh, honey," Jane said. "You *do* have a family of your own."

"*We're* your family," Molly said.

"I know." But an aunt and a cousin were not the same as a husband and children. And all three women knew it.

"Anyway," Chloe said, sighing again—good grief, she was doing a lot of sighing. "That's part of what's been keeping me awake the last two nights."

"Last *two* nights," Jane said, frowning as Chloe's words sank in. "You mean you've known about Todd's marriage to Meredith since Thursday?"

Chloe nodded.

"And you didn't *call* me?" Molly squeaked.

"I'm sorry. I…wanted to settle some things in my mind first." Chloe knew she'd probably hurt her cousin's feelings—after all, in addition to being cousins they were best friends and had been since they were toddlers. Molly was two years younger than Chloe, but the difference in their ages had never mattered to them. "One thing I did figure out is that there are probably going to be some rough patches ahead."

"Look, honey," her aunt said, reaching over to pat

Chloe's hand, "I know it's hard right now, but you're a strong person…you'll weather this…and in the end, I believe you'll be better off."

Just get it over with. Tell them. "There's something else."

Jane and Molly both frowned. Chloe could almost see the wheels turning.

"I'm pregnant."

For one long moment, the only sounds in the kitchen were the ticking of the wall clock and the humming of the refrigerator. Then cousin and aunt spoke at once.

"Oh, Chloe."

"Oh, dear."

Chloe sighed. Nodded. "Yep."

"Does…does Todd know?" This came from Molly.

"No."

"Why not?"

"I'm only about three—at the most four—weeks along. I had no idea when he left. And then, when I suspected and had it confirmed with a pregnancy test—actually, *two* pregnancy tests—I wanted to wait to tell him in person." At this, tears threatened, but Chloe forced them back.

Molly's gaze met hers steadily. "So when do you plan to tell him now?"

"I don't."

"You *don't?*" Jane asked.

"No."

"But, honey—"

"Don't tell me he has a right to know, Aunt Jane. As far as I'm concerned, Todd Hopewell has forfeited any rights he ever had with me."

"But, Chloe, he's the baby's father. Don't you think—"

"No, I *don't* think."

Chloe saw how Molly's glance darted to her mother, then hurriedly returned to Chloe. "I don't blame you," she said. "In your shoes, I'd probably feel the same way."

"Thank you," Chloe said. She looked at her aunt.

Her aunt sighed. "You know I'll support you no matter what you ultimately decide."

"I've already decided. And I won't change my mind."

"I just…well, I don't see how you can keep your baby a secret from him. Riverton's a small town. He's bound to find out you've had a baby. Don't you think he'll put two and two together? And then what?"

"He won't find out."

"Chloe, of *course* he'll find out…"

"I'm moving away."

"What?" Molly looked stricken.

Jane was shaking her head. "Chloe, sweetheart, you can't move away."

"Of course I can. It's easy. There's no problem with the townhouse—I mean, because of the wedding I'd already given my notice."

"But, sweetie," Jane said, "where will you go?"

"I thought Syracuse."

"You'll hate Syracuse," Molly said. "You know how much you dislike traffic and crowds."

"I'll get used to the differences. Besides, I don't plan to live downtown or anything like that. I hope to buy or rent a little house out in the suburbs. Don't look so unhappy. You can come see me whenever you want, and

I'll visit here, too. As long as I'm not out and about in Riverton, there's very little chance Todd will find out about the baby."

"How soon are you planning to go?" Jane asked. Her forehead was still creased with concern.

"By July 1st, I thought."

"So soon?" Molly said.

"Well, I figured I'd begin showing in August. No sense in taking any chances."

"I hate this," Molly said. "And it's all that jerk's fault!" If looks could kill, Todd would bite the dust.

"Have you seen a doctor yet?" Jane asked.

Chloe shook her head. "I was planning to ask Todd's mother who she'd recommend. I thought that might be a way to win her over…if I asked for her advice." So much for *that* plan.

"You are planning to see someone soon, aren't you? Just to confirm everything and get prenatal vitamins and everything," Jane said. "I mean, you're not going to wait until you move."

"I honestly hadn't thought that far ahead," Chloe said. Lord, there were so many things to think about. "But yes, I guess I should see someone here first. Is there anyone you'd recommend?"

"Go to Dr. Ramsey," Molly said. "She's Sylvia's ob-gyn, and Sylvia loves her. Says she's wonderful." Sylvia Alvarez was a coworker at the school where Molly taught.

"I still wish—" Jane started.

"Aunt Jane," Chloe said, "I know what you wish. I wish it, too. I don't want to leave Riverton any more than you and Molly want me to, but I see no other way. The Hopewell family has made it very clear they want nothing to do with me. And now I want nothing to do with them. I'm not taking any chances with my baby. And if that means I have to move away, so be it."

Just before noon, Chloe was in the middle of a particularly intricate Web-site design when the doorbell rang. "Damn," she mumbled. She wasn't expecting any deliveries today. She considered ignoring the caller, but like the phone, she found the doorbell almost impossible to ignore. After nudging Samson out of the way, she headed toward the hallway.

The doorbell rang again as she approached the front door. "I'm coming." She could see a man's jeans-clad leg in the left glass panel at the side of the door. Frowning, she peered into the peephole. Startled by the sight of Simon Hopewell's face, she jerked back.

Todd's brother! What in the world was *he* doing there?

Smoothing down her knit shirt and khaki cargo pants, she opened the door.

"Hello, Chloe."

"Hello, Simon." Her heart was beating a little too fast, and it irritated her that just the sight of a member of Todd's family could rattle her.

"May I come in?"

His gray eyes, which reminded her of the color of clouds on a rainy day, looked troubled. What was *he* worried about? He wasn't the one who'd practically been stood up at the altar. He wasn't the one who was pregnant—but of course he knew nothing about that.

Did he think she might sue the family or something? She shrugged. "I suppose so."

"I'm sorry to bother you during the day. I know you work at home. But I really needed to see you."

By now he had stepped into the entryway.

Grudgingly, she admitted to herself that Simon Hopewell seemed like a nice person. Unlike his mother, he'd certainly never been anything but kind to her.

Resigned, she led him into her small living room. Indicating the sofa, she said, "Have a seat. Can I get you something to drink? Iced tea? Water? Coffee?"

"Thank you, no. I'm fine." He sat on the end of the sofa, and she sat in the bentwood rocking chair on the other side of the room.

"I just wanted to tell you how sorry I am about everything that's happened."

"Thank you."

"I also wanted you to know that my brother's actions disgust me, and I've told him so."

Chloe could just imagine what Todd thought about that. He'd told her often enough how overbearing Simon was. "He thinks he knows everything," he'd said more than once. "Always trying to tell me what to do."

"One of the things that worries me is I know you've incurred wedding expenses."

Chloe thought about the wedding gown hanging in her closet upstairs. The fact she'd bought it off the sale rack at Bloomingdale's didn't soften the reality that she'd paid more than eight hundred dollars for it. The veil had been another three hundred and fifty. Perhaps it could be returned. The dress couldn't; it had been altered to fit her. Thank goodness she hadn't paid the deposit on the country club. That had been Todd's doing because he's the one who had wanted to hold the reception there. Chloe would have been happy with a small reception in the church hall after the ceremony.

And then there were the deposits for the church, the flowers, the cake, the material for Molly's dress and the photographer. Oh, well. Thank goodness she hadn't charged anything. Everything had been paid for in cash. So even though she was out the money, at least she wasn't in debt.

Simon reached into the pocket of his pale blue shirt, pulled out a folded check and placed it on the coffee table. "Five thousand should cover everything, I think. If you need more, just let me know."

"I don't want your money."

"And I don't want you paying for my brother's bad behavior."

"I'll just tear the check up." No way she was taking his money. Hopewell money. Bad enough she was keeping the ring. She had no intention of being indebted to the Hopewells for anything else. "Look, this isn't your problem. And the Hopewell family...*your* family... owes me nothing."

"I understand why you might feel that way. Frankly, if I were you, I wouldn't want to have anything to do with my family, either. But why don't I just leave the check? After thinking about it, you might change your mind. I hope you do."

She shook her head. "I won't. But thank you for making the offer."

He leaned forward. Neither said anything. For a long moment, the only sound was a faraway siren outside. Finally, his thoughtful gaze met hers. "Are you doing okay?"

She sat up straighter. "I'm just fine. In fact, I'm more than fine." Her chin lifted. "This has all actually worked out better for me. Now I can do something I've wanted to do for a long time. I'm moving away from Riverton."

He stared at her. "I'm really sorry to hear that."

Why was he looking at her that way? His steady gaze was unsettling. She wished she knew what he was thinking. "Don't be. I told you. I've wanted to make a change in my life, and this is the perfect time."

He nodded thoughtfully. Seemed about to say something else, but didn't. Instead he rose. "Well, in that case, I won't impose on you any longer. Thank you for seeing me. And again, please accept my apology for the way you've been treated. I hope you won't judge our entire family by my brother's immaturity and actions."

Something about the sincere manner in which he offered the apology touched Chloe in a way she wouldn't have expected. Simon Hopewell really was a nice person. A good person. In fact, he was nothing like the way Todd had often described him. She realized Todd had probably always been jealous—and probably resentful—of his older brother.

She walked Simon to the front door, and just before he walked outside, he turned back to her and said, "I meant what I said before. If you need anything—anything at all—just call me."

Chloe never would have believed she would feel both

guilt and regret over her decision to keep her baby a secret from the Hopewell family. But seeing the sincerity and genuine concern for her welfare in Simon Hopewell's eyes left her awash in both emotions as he walked away.

Yet she knew she would not change her mind.

And no matter what hardships faced her in the future, she would never pick up the phone and call Simon.

She was finished with the Hopewell family.

Chapter Three

Simon was impressed by Chloe's refusal to take the money he'd offered. He'd always suspected the Hopewell money had nothing to do with her engagement to Todd, even as his mother insisted the money *had* to be an influence.

"After all, the girl comes from nothing," she'd said more than once. "She couldn't *help* but be dazzled by our money."

Well, she *wasn't* dazzled. And it would give Simon a great deal of satisfaction to make sure his mother knew it. Not that knowing of Chloe's integrity would change his mother's mind about her. Simon actually understood where his mother was coming from, even as he abhorred her inability to rise above her own humble beginnings. Larissa would happily die rather than have her so-called friends know about the way she'd grown up. In her skewed way of thinking, she felt she had to avoid any contact with lesser mortals lest she be tarred by the same brush.

It was sad, Simon thought, that even after all these years, his mother was still so basically insecure. Yet for all his understanding of its origins, Larissa's continued snobbery exasperated him, especially when it was directed at someone like Chloe, who had overcome tougher circumstances than Larissa *ever* had to face.

Simon had also been impressed by Chloe's dignity. In her shoes, he'd be angry, maybe even vindictive. But if she felt either of those emotions, she had certainly hidden them well.

Christ, his brother was a fool. If the lovely, green-eyed Chloe had belonged to him, Simon would have made sure he hung on to her. And his family be damned! Not that there was anything wrong with Meredith. She was a nice enough person, smart even—she'd been doing a good job as Todd's assistant—but in Simon's opinion she couldn't hold a candle to Chloe. Of course, *Meredith's* parents belonged to the Riverton Country Club, and Paul Belson, her father, was the town's most prominent lawyer.

As he drove to the office—Saturday or not, Simon had work to catch up on—he kept thinking about his brother's former fiancée. The way she'd treated him so politely yet firmly, the way her determined eyes met his directly when she refused the money, the way she said the Hopewell family owed her nothing.

That's the reason it bothered him when she said she

was leaving Riverton, he decided. Maybe she was more affected by Todd's desertion than she would have him believe.

Yet she didn't seem the type to run away. She definitely had given him the impression she was a stand-and-fight young woman—not the kind who would turn tail and run. Even so, something was making her leave Riverton, and Simon wasn't sure he bought her reasoning. So he would keep tabs on her for a while…just to make sure she really was okay.

He'd just arrived at this decision when he pulled into his parking slot at the company's headquarters. Glancing over, he spotted Mark DelVecchio's red Porsche. Mark was his CFO, and like Simon, he often worked on Saturdays. Other than Mark's car, the security guard's car and the cleaning crew's van, the parking lot was empty. Well, Simon didn't blame his staff for wanting to spend a balmy spring day on the golf course or puttering around their houses. This part of upstate New York could still be experiencing a wintry chill in May— in fact, he could remember a few years back when they'd gotten a late snowfall in early May—so a day in the seventies was one to savor.

"Hey, Russ, how's it going?" he said to the security guard as he walked past his station by the front entrance.

"Good, Mr. Hopewell, good. How about you?"

"I'm great. How's Erin?" The guard's fourteen-year-old daughter had fallen earlier in the month and broken her arm.

"She's doin' okay. Hates rehab, though. Complains about it constantly."

"Don't blame her." Simon remembered his own stint with rehab after a soccer injury in college. "Physical therapy can be tough." He smiled. "Give your family my best."

"I'll do that."

Pleasantries over, Simon headed for the stairs. Bypassing the elevator, he jogged up to the third floor. He was whistling as he walked down the hall toward his corner office.

"Hey, Simon!" Mark DelVecchio called out.

Stopping, Simon looked into Mark's office. Dressed in khaki shorts, a brown golf shirt and deck shoes, Mark leaned back in his leather swivel chair with his feet propped on his desk. "You should be home with Deanna and the girls today," Simon said.

"Yeah, I know, but I wanted to go over the budget forecast again."

Simon didn't like the somber note in Mark's voice.

"Look, Simon, I know you won't be happy about this, but I've looked at everything, and I'm afraid there's no way we can pay bonuses this year."

Simon nodded unhappily. He'd arrived at the same conclusion. "Maybe if the contract with Petry comes through…"

"I don't think it's going to."

Simon hated to admit it, but Mark was probably right. The contract that had once looked so promising now looked as if it might bite the dust. And that disappointment could be laid directly at Todd's door. If he'd been here the way he was *supposed* to be to coddle the prospect along—after all, he was the one they knew—

maybe the outcome would be different. "The department heads count on those bonuses," he said, although Mark knew that as well as Simon did. "They'll be really upset."

"I know, but it's either that or put off retooling indefinitely."

Retooling of the plant was essential, Simon felt. His father had ignored the signs of change and refused to face facts. It wasn't until after his death that Simon had been able to even talk to the board of directors about modernizing the plant. They weren't happy about spending the kind of money necessary but had finally agreed the company wouldn't be able to compete in the new global marketplace unless they did. "We can't put off the retooling," he finally said.

For the rest of the afternoon, he studied the company's financial reports, his department heads' budgets, the salary forecasts. He looked at the latest bills from the insurance underwriters—rates for both health and life insurance for the employees and their families and fire and hazard insurance for the buildings and equipment had increased again.

His reluctant conclusion was that although the company was in good shape, in order to meet their long-term goals, some sacrifices were unavoidable.

Simon put his head in his hands.

Sometimes he hated his job.

Chloe hadn't been able to get Simon Hopewell's visit out of her mind. For the next few days, she kept thinking about him. He and Todd were so different. Yes, they both had black hair and the square-jawed look of all the

Hopewells, but the resemblance ended there. Todd's eyes were a bright blue, and most of the time they betrayed exactly what he was thinking, whereas Simon's eyes were an enigmatic, cool gray. Contemplative, serious eyes.

Todd smiled easily and often—was charming and friendly. Simon was just the opposite—almost stern in his quiet, businesslike demeanor. He rarely smiled and, according to Todd, had no sense of humor at all. Of course, Chloe thought wryly, Todd had made other pronouncements that had turned out not to be true.

Todd liked to spend money. All through their courtship, he was constantly buying gifts and taking her to expensive places. Simon, on the other hand—again, according to Todd—kept an iron fist on the purse strings.

Despite this, Simon had generously offered to take care of all the wedding expenses, and his eyes were kind when he made his offer. Certainly Chloe never felt as if he were condescending to her the way his mother had. It had almost seemed like a point of honor with him.

What would Simon Hopewell think if he knew about the baby she was carrying? Would he be upset? Would he think she had tried to trap Todd? Maybe so. She hated thinking that might be the case. She almost wished she could tell him.

But that was ridiculous. She could never tell him. Chloe wondered why, suddenly, she felt such a twinge of regret. She told herself it was only because Simon would make such a great uncle, someone her baby could definitely depend upon and look up to.

She did feel regret about the fact there would be a

lack of male influence in her baby's life. Her father's death, her uncle Phil's death in Iraq—there would be no Patterson men to count on. And now, because of Todd's betrayal, there would be no Hopewell men, either.

Well, it couldn't be helped. What was done was done and could not be undone. Nor did she want it to be. Now that Todd had revealed his true colors, she knew she was better off without him, for the one character trait Chloe valued above all others was honesty. A trait Todd obviously did not possess.

So…good riddance to bad rubbish, as Grandmother Patterson used to say. Chloe and her baby would be just fine on their own. Better than fine. They would be great. But even as she told herself all this, tears slid down her face, and all the doubts and fears she'd thought she'd successfully buried tried to resurface. Angrily, she brushed away the tears. *I'm fine. I'm strong. I can do anything.*

Her words were an affirmation, one she'd repeated often throughout her life. And just as they had before they made her feel better.

Composed now, she headed for the kitchen.

A nice bowl of Ben & Jerry's Chocolate Chip Cookie Dough wouldn't hurt, either.

Simon put off going to see his mother until Wednesday. He knew it was cowardly, but he was tired of scenes and this one promised to be a doozy. But since there was a board meeting scheduled for Thursday afternoon, he knew he had to tell her the bad news before then. He called the house Wednesday morning and said he planned to drop by in the afternoon if she were going to be home.

"As it happens, my bridge club was changed to yesterday, so I'll be here," his mother said.

"I'll see you around four, then."

Simon marshaled his arguments on the drive out to the family home. When he pulled into the circular drive in front of the stately three-story colonial, he knew he was as ready as he ever would be to face the coming storm.

"I've asked Martha to bring tea into the solarium," his mother said as she ushered him in. Martha was their longtime housekeeper.

The solarium was Simon's favorite room in the house. On the east side of the house, morning sun poured in its windows. His mother had filled the room with lots of greenery and dozens of her prized orchids, as well as a fountain and waterfall at one end of the room. Percy, his mother's pet parrot, occupied a fancy gilded cage in the shaded northwest corner, and Max, her chocolate Lab, could usually be found lying in front of the windows overlooking the river that meandered along the back of their property. Although the rest of the house was furnished with expensive antiques and imported rugs, the solarium was casually and cheerfully filled with bamboo chairs and sofas covered with bright chintz cushions. Dotted around the room were glass-topped side tables and a matching tea wagon. Today, because the day was mild, some of the windows were open, and Simon could hear the snip of the gardener's shears somewhere nearby.

"I'm glad you called," Larissa said, settling into her favorite chair by the waterfall. Max slowly got to his feet, stretched and moved over to her side, where he noisily flopped down once more. "I wanted to talk to you about the board meeting, anyway."

"What about it?"

His mother started to speak, then fell silent as Martha entered the room carrying a large silver tray. She set it down on the tea wagon, then wheeled the wagon close to where his mother was seated. The tray was loaded with a silver teapot, creamer, sugar bowl, cups and saucers, small plates and a platter filled with bite-size sandwiches and a matching cake dish upon which sat what looked like a lemon sponge cake—Simon's favorite.

He smiled at Martha. "How'd you know I was coming today?"

Her answering smile was warm. "Don't you know I'm a mind reader?"

"Among other things," he said, laughing. *Like a saint for putting up with our family all these years.*

Once Martha left the room and Simon and his mother had helped themselves to the refreshments, his mother said, "I wanted to discuss the amount of the family allocations before we talked about them at the meeting."

"That's why I came today. To talk about them."

His mother raised her eyebrows. "Oh?" She lifted her teacup and sipped, her blue eyes meeting his over the rim of the cup.

Simon knew there was no percentage in stalling. He drank some of his own tea, then put the cup down and leaned forward. "I wish I had better news for you, Mom. I know what I have to say will not be pleasant to hear, but the bottom line is, there will be no increases to any of the family allocations this year."

Setting her own cup down a trifle harder than the fine china warranted, his mother's gaze turned icy. "You're not serious. You couldn't possibly be. Of course we must have an increase. Perhaps *you* don't need one, but I simply can't continue on without one, and I know Todd will feel the same way. After all, he's just been married. It's outrageous to think he can continue to live on the same amount of money. First of all, he and Meredith cannot live indefinitely in that *condo* of his." She said the word *condo* as if it caused a bad taste in her mouth. "It's tacky, all that black and red and chrome, just not the kind of place a young woman like Meredith would ever want to live in. I mean, surely you can see that, if anything, Todd will need to have his allocation *doubled!*"

There were a few things Simon could say to that, like the fact that in addition to his share of profits, Todd also drew a substantial salary from the company, but he'd learned long ago how futile it was to criticize his youngest brother. "I wish the company could afford to give *everyone* an increase—whether a family member or an employee— but Mark and I have gone over the numbers, and the company is simply not in a position to do so this year."

"That's ridiculous. I absolutely must have more to live on. If you think it's easy to run this big house on what you give me…you're mistaken. I make sacrifices to do so, and I'm tired of going without. I need at least fifty thousand more this year. I'd *like* seventy thousand, but I suppose I can manage on fifty." She sat back in her chair with a satisfied smile. The queen bestowing a favor on one of her subjects. "No, Max," she added irritably, as the dog nudged her leg. "Cake is bad for you."

Simon suppressed a sigh. "Mother, the money is not what *I* give you. As one of the principal owners of Hopewell Enterprises the money is your share of each year's profits. This year, there is very little profit. What with the new equipment, increases in some other expenses and the coming cost of retooling the plant, we're stretched to the limit. In fact, your allocation should be cut by more than half. I realize that would cause you enormous hardship, so I plan to ask the board to okay keeping the amount the same as last year's with the provision that we'll take another look in six months."

Larissa's face paled. "And what does *that* mean?"

"It means if the changes we've made don't help us improve our bottom line the way we think they will, we might have to decrease the amount you're getting now." Simon delivered this news as gently as he could.

"*Decrease* my share? *Decrease* it?" She jumped up. "How *dare* you!" She glared at him. "My own *son!* I can't believe I'm hearing this. Why, your father would turn over in his grave if he knew how you were treating me. Weren't you *listening* to me? I can't run this house on what I'm getting *now,* let alone on *less.* What's wrong with you, Simon? I'm beginning to think you've lost your mind. Either that or the power of running the company has gone to your head. The board will never go along with this. Never! In fact, I'm going to call Elias as soon as you leave here."

Elias Whitney was president of the board and, along with Larissa, one of the largest shareholders in the company. He had, also along with Larissa, been against many of the changes Simon had recommended, although, in the end, he'd gone along with them.

Her threat didn't scare Simon. Elias Whitney might be a longtime family friend, but he was also a shrewd businessman. Ultimately, he would continue to vote for the financial health of the company.

"Hopefully, this situation is only temporary. Just until we pay for all the upgrades."

"Simon, are you hard of hearing? Have you not heard a word I said? I don't have enough money to live on unless I get an increase. What do you propose I do? Do you want me to sell this house? Is that it?"

"I know you don't want to sell the house." Although why she needed an eight-bedroom home was beyond him. It wasn't as if any of them still lived with her. Simon had bought his own home ten years ago, and both Todd and Noah had moved out years earlier. "But you *could* sell some of your stock to tide you over."

"My *stock!*" She looked as shocked as if he'd suggested she sell her body. She gave him a hard look. "You *have* lost your mind. I will *never* sell my stock. That's my insurance for the future."

Simon knew that his father had carried a five-million dollar policy on his life and that most of that money should still be intact. Plus her company stock was worth upward of twenty million dollars, so her future was completely secure. But his mother was angry enough; he didn't want to make things worse by pointing out the obvious.

For a few moments, he considered offering his mother the money she wanted—not as a loan but as a gift. Simon could afford it. He lived simply and saved more than he spent, and the value of his company stock was equal to hers. But he was reluctant for some reason. If she really did have money problems, he would have gladly helped her out. But she didn't. She was just spoiled…and had a sense of entitlement. In her mind, since throughout her life as a Hopewell she'd always had whatever she wanted, she always *should* have whatever she wanted.

Maybe it was past time for her to learn what most people were forced to learn: that there was a difference between *want* and *need.*

An hour later, they were still going round and round with the same arguments. Finally, Simon rose. "Look, we're not getting anywhere like this. I'm sorry you're so upset, but I can't change things just because you want them changed. And I think tomorrow's board meeting will bear me out." Max had gotten up when Simon did, and Simon rubbed his head.

"You haven't heard the last of this, Simon. I'm not giving up. I intend to call Elias and then I'll call all the other board members, as well."

"That's your right, Mother."

"And then we'll just *see* who's boss."

"Yes, I guess we will."

She didn't kiss him goodbye when he left. In fact, she barely said goodbye. He knew she was furious, and he had a feeling she'd be even more furious tomorrow, because he would bet his entire stock portfolio on the fact that the board members would vote with him and Mark. They couldn't afford not to. Hopewell's entire future depended on them making sensible financial decisions, and investing now for the future of the company was the most sensible financial decision they could possibly make.

But Simon wasn't rejoicing in his anticipated victory. How could he?

His mother might be spoiled. She might have a misguided sense of entitlement. And she might sometimes be unreasonable and petty. But he remembered how she'd always read him a bedtime story, even when she and his father were going out for the evening, how when he was miserable with chicken pox she'd played card games with him for days on end, how she'd beamed with pride when he'd given the valedictory address upon his graduation from college.

No matter what, she was his mother, and he loved her.

As he drove home, he remembered that he'd meant to tell her about his visit to Chloe and how she'd turned down his offer to pay the wedding expenses. But under the circumstances, maybe it was a good thing he hadn't mentioned Todd's ex-fiancée. His mother was upset enough.

No sense adding fuel to the fire.

Chapter Four

The board meeting went exactly as Simon had expected. All the directors, Elias Whitney in particular, were sympathetic to Larissa's point of view, but in good conscience, they couldn't vote the increase she wanted. Elias apologized to her, but Simon's mother—after glaring at him—stormed out of the meeting in a fury.

"I'm sorry," Elias said to Simon afterward. "I know this is going to make things uncomfortable for you."

Simon shrugged. Things were already uncomfortable. And none of it was Elias's fault. If only Larissa's anger was the only reaction Simon had to face. Unfortunately, hers was just the beginning of the storm. By Friday afternoon—after spending hours breaking the bad news of no bonuses to his management staff—Simon wished there was a hole somewhere he could crawl into. At the very least, he wanted a glass of wine and a good dinner. And maybe a weekend of golf. How long had it been since he'd actually taken a weekend for himself?

As he left the office, he thought about how nice it would be if the good dinner was even now being prepared by a beautiful wife, someone who would understand and sympathize with him and tell him he'd only done what he had to do. Someone who would later join him in his king-size bed. And why was it that this thought immediately segued into one of Chloe Patterson?

What was wrong with him? In the past few days, he'd hardly stopped thinking about Todd's former fiancée. Sure, she was attractive, but Simon knew dozens of attractive women, and he didn't think about *them* all the time. What was it about Chloe that refused to leave him alone?

Simon was too honest with himself to blame his preoccupation with her on the fact Todd had jilted her. The truth was, she intrigued him on a personal level. Hell, if he were being *completely* honest, he'd admit that he was attracted to her...sexually attracted. Maybe he had been from the first time he met her. He still remembered the way he'd felt when he saw her with Todd at the company's Christmas party last year. Jealous. Almost resentful. It had ticked him off to see Todd with the fresh-faced Chloe with the spectacular legs—she'd worn a short, dark red dress that swirled when she walked—when he, Simon, was alone that night.

Remembering how he'd felt then, he could feel his body responding now. Damn. He'd been without a woman for too long. In fact, he and Alexis had broken up a few weeks before that Christmas party. It was the reason he was alone that night.

He told himself he was being ridiculous obsessing over his brother's former fiancée. What he needed to do was say yes to one of the dozens of invitations that came his way from more appropriate potential romantic partners. Because Chloe was off-limits. And even if she hadn't been, she was planning to leave Riverton. Any involvement with her would be a go-nowhere situation—a real exercise in frustration.

But even as he told himself all this, he wondered what she'd say if he were to call her and ask her to have dinner with him. The desire to do so was so strong that he almost reached for his cell. But common sense quickly intervened. *Hell, I'll just be asking for problems. She'll say no, anyway, so why open that can of worms?*

Despite his rationally thought out decision, ten minutes later he found himself driving past Rosa's Trattoria, one of the most popular restaurants in Riverton. He remembered from the investigator's report that Chloe and her cousin and aunt had a habit of meeting there for dinner on Friday nights.

Would they be there tonight?

Glancing through the parking lot, he spied Chloe's distinctive lime-green Volkswagen. Knowing this was stupid, that he should go somewhere else, he pulled into the lot and parked.

"Mr. Hopewell!" Gino Carbone, husband to Rosa and co-owner of the restaurant, exclaimed as Simon walked in. "Welcome back. How are you?"

"I'm fine, Gino. And you?"

"Excellent, excellent. It's been a while since you've been here."

"Too long," Simon agreed.

"Are you expecting someone or—"

"It's just me tonight." Simon tried to keep from looking into the dining room, but out of the corner of his eye he could see Chloe sitting with two women at a nearby table.

Gino picked up a menu and beckoned Simon to follow him. Simon knew they would have to pass by Chloe's table. A moment later, Chloe looked up. When their eyes met, hers reflected her surprise, but she quickly smiled and gave him a friendly hello.

He stopped, smiling back. "Hello, Chloe. How nice to see you again." She looked beautiful in a green blouse that exactly matched her eyes.

When he continued to stand there, she only hesitated a few seconds before introducing him to her companions. "Aunt Jane, Molly, I'd like you to meet Simon Hopewell. Simon is Todd's oldest brother."

Simon grimaced. "But please don't hold that against me."

Jane Patterson, an attractive dark-haired woman, chuckled. "It's nice to meet you, Mr. Hopewell." Her brown eyes were filled with curiosity and intelligence. Simon knew she was taking his measure as she studied him. The cousin, a pretty young woman with curly dark hair who was about Chloe's age, studied him carefully, too.

Protective, he thought. Both of them. And probably suspicious, too. Well, he could hardly blame them. Up till now, Chloe hadn't fared well at the hands of the Hopewells.

Chloe's aunt offered her hand, and Simon shook it, then turned to Molly and shook hers, as well. He knew they wouldn't invite him to join them, but at least he would get to observe them awhile, for they hadn't been served yet.

But Chloe surprised him and—from the expression on their faces—also surprised her aunt and cousin by saying, "Are you all by yourself tonight?"

"I'm afraid so," he replied.

"Um, would you like to join us? We've placed our orders, but we haven't eaten yet."

Simon knew he should refuse. Well, hell, he shouldn't even *be* here, should he? Instead, he said, "Are you sure you don't mind?"

At this, Chloe hesitated, glancing at her aunt.

"Do join us, Mr. Hopewell," her aunt said.

"Thank you, then. I'd love to. But please…call me Simon."

Gino pulled another chair over to the table, and Simon sat down. He was seated directly across from Chloe, who now seemed uncomfortable. Probably regretting her impulsive invitation, he thought. "This is really nice of you," he said, addressing the remark to Jane.

"I know how much I hate eating alone," she said.

"It does get old."

"I eat alone all the time," Molly said, her voice stiff.

For a moment, an awkward silence fell. Then Chloe said, "Todd left some of his belongings at my place. Um, would you mind sending someone from the office to pick them up?"

Simon shook his head. "I'll come and get them myself. Will you be home tomorrow?"

"Yes."

"What time would be best?"

"It doesn't matter. Whatever's convenient for you."

"How about if I give you a call in the morning? We can set a time then."

"All right."

Simon was mentally berating Todd. But this was typical Todd behavior. He rarely considered anyone else's feelings. Despite this, he continued to charm most people.

"You have another brother besides Todd, don't you?" This came from Jane, who probably just wanted to switch to a less uncomfortable topic.

"Yes, I do. Noah."

"I think I've met him at the shelter. Does he often do volunteer work there?"

"It's more than a volunteer job," Simon said. "He's the assistant director. Works at the shelter full-time."

"Really? You have a most unusual family, Mr. Hope—"

"Simon," he said.

She smiled. "Simon."

Simon shrugged. "No more so than most families."

"Most young men born to privilege wouldn't dream of working at a homeless shelter."

"That's probably true, but Noah's the one who's unusual. Otherwise, my family is pretty typical."

"Oh, come on, you're being modest. Wasn't your uncle on the New York Court of Appeals?"

"Yes."

"And wasn't your grandfather an ambassador to England?"

Most people only knew that the Hopewell family owned the largest corporation in the area and were wealthy. "That's right. You seem to know a lot about my family."

"Chloe is very important to me. You don't think I'd've let her marry into a family without checking them out thoroughly, do you? As I'm sure you checked out Chloe and *her* family."

Touché, Simon thought. Nothing much would get past this woman.

"You're right again. I did have a thorough investigation done when Todd became engaged to Chloe." Turning to Chloe, he added, "Sorry about that." He wished he could explain why, but this wasn't the time or the place.

Chloe gave him a crooked smile. "I figured as much. Actually, I thought your *mother* would do it. Seeing as how she hates me." This last statement was said bitterly.

"She doesn't hate you."

"Well, she certainly doesn't like me. She made that clear enough. I'll bet she's overjoyed I'll no longer have to be a part of your family."

"She treated Chloe terribly," Molly said, anger written all over her expressive face.

Simon wanted to deny both these statements, too, but all three women would know he was lying if he did. He shifted uncomfortably and, for the first time, wished he hadn't said yes to the invitation to join them. They were probably all wishing the same thing.

"So what did your investigator tell you?" Chloe asked, her voice cooler now.

"I know you came to live with your aunt after your father died."

"And I'm sure your investigator also told you about my mother," Chloe said. Her chin went up defiantly.

Simon liked her courage. She obviously wasn't afraid to confront the truth. "Yes," he said quietly.

"We loved having Chloe with us," Jane said, reaching over and taking Chloe's hand. "She's another daughter to me."

"Best thing that ever happened to us," Molly echoed. She gave him a look even more defiant than Chloe's had been. It said, *I dare you to say anything different.*

"And I loved being with you," Chloe said.

Nearby someone cleared his throat. "Are you ready to order, Mr. Hopewell?"

Simon looked up, glad for the interruption. Nick, Gino's son, had been standing a few feet away, patiently waiting for a lull in their conversation. Simon just hoped he hadn't heard what they'd been talking about. "Sorry, Nick. Yes, I'll have the lasagna and—" he turned back to the Patterson women "—would you ladies like a glass of wine? I'd like to order a bottle for the table."

"That sounds lovely," Jane said.

"No wine for me," Chloe said. "I'll just stick with iced tea."

Molly remained quiet, her entire stance saying she still didn't trust him. Not one little bit.

Simon wished he could reassure Chloe's cousin that he would never do anything to hurt Chloe. That he wasn't his idiot brother. That he realized Chloe's value. But this wasn't the time or the place. And the truth was, he didn't blame Molly for her attitude. It was deserved. He felt bad that he'd probably ruined her evening.

But maybe he could salvage something for them. He would certainly pay for everyone's dinner. With that in mind, Simon also ordered the fried calamari appetizer. "To share," he said to Nick, "and bring us some of the bruschetta, too." Within minutes, Nick was back with a bottle of pinot noir. "The calamari, bruschetta and your salads will be out in a few minutes," he said as he poured the wine.

"You sure you don't want some?" Simon said to Chloe.

"I'm sure."

"To the future," Jane said as she raised her glass in a toast. Chloe and Simon quickly followed, but Molly just sat there.

Jane didn't say anything, but she gave her daughter a look. Molly flushed and finally lifted her glass, too.

"And new beginnings," Chloe said, her voice determinedly upbeat.

Jane frowned. "I wish we could change your mind about that new beginning." She turned to Simon. "Did she tell you she's planning to move away from Riverton?"

"Yes. I take it you're not happy about it."

"Not happy at all!" Molly said, glaring at him.

Simon cringed inwardly. Man, that girl would cheerfully annihilate him if she could.

Chloe rubbed at the condensation on her glass. "I'm sorry. But I won't change my mind."

Jane sighed. "She's so stubborn."

"Why *are* you moving?" Simon asked.

"I told you," Chloe said, looking away. "It's time for a change."

Simon studied her for a moment, wishing she'd meet his eyes. "I can't help thinking if it hadn't been for Todd that you wouldn't be going anywhere."

"Todd has nothing to do with my decision," she said. This time her eyes *did* meet his. In them he saw a challenge and something else. Something he couldn't put his finger on.

Simon wished what she'd said was true, but he was sure it wasn't. He glanced at Jane, saw that she was studying Chloe thoughtfully, too. He'd love to know what she was thinking. What they *all* were thinking.

Silence fell again as Simon cast about for a different topic of conversation. Before he could introduce one, their salads arrived along with the bruschetta, the platter of calamari and a bowl of marinara sauce for dipping. After that, they busied themselves with the food, and when the conversation resumed, some of the tension seemed to have dissolved. Thank God, Simon thought. Even Molly seemed to relax, as the women discussed possible vacation spots for her and some fellow teachers who were planning to do something together after summer school was over in late July. Simon didn't say much, using the time instead to study Chloe and her relationship with her family.

Todd was an even greater fool than Simon had initially thought. Chloe was a jewel, and Simon couldn't help but think Todd might be sorry one day. Yet Simon was no longer angry with his brother. Because Chloe was definitely better off. Now she would be free to find someone better, someone more deserving of her.

Simon's only regret was that it couldn't be him.

* * *

Chloe finally relaxed, although she still couldn't imagine why she'd invited Simon to join them. It was the last thing she'd intended, yet the words were out of her mouth before she realized what she was going to say.

But there was no harm in this, she told herself. It was just a meal. After tomorrow, when Simon stopped by for Todd's belongings, she would never have to see him again. Soon she would be gone from Riverton—and beyond the reach of the Hopewells.

Finishing her salad, she took a drink of her iced tea, and her glance moved to the arched doorway of the dining room where a party of women were waiting to be seated. *Ohmigod.* Her heart lurched as her brain registered the identity of the tallest of the four women. It was Larissa Hopewell. Chloe's mouth went dry, and her gaze darted to Simon, who was saying something to Jane.

Out of the corner of her eye, Chloe could see Gino lead the women into the room. They would have to walk right by Chloe's table. There was no way Simon's mother wouldn't see them. *Oh, boy,* Chloe thought. *This should be interesting. I just hope Molly doesn't go ballistic.* Chloe wished she could warn Simon, but he wasn't looking at her, and she didn't want to be obvious.

She *felt* rather than saw the party of women stop at their table. A moment later, Simon felt them, too, for he looked around.

There was an instant of silence, an instant that felt like an eternity to Chloe. Jane reached under the table and squeezed Chloe's knee, and on the other side of her, Molly visibly stiffened.

"Well," Larissa Hopewell said. The word might have been carved in ice. "Good evening, Simon."

"Hello, Mother." Simon nodded at the others. "Nice to see you, Mrs. Barnes, Mrs. Whitney, Mrs. Belson."

Oh, God. Not just Larissa Hopewell, but Meredith's mother! The other two women murmured politely, but Chloe knew their minds were probably spinning, just as hers was. Meredith's mother, a lovely looking woman with red hair who strongly resembled her daughter, looked as if she'd rather be anywhere but there. No one could have missed the coolness of Larissa's greeting, and Chloe was sure that both Margaret Barnes and Mrs. Belson knew who she was. Deciding it was best to take the high road, she said, "Hello, Mrs. Hopewell," in as pleasant a voice as she could manage. "I'd like to introduce my aunt, Jane Patterson, and my cousin, Molly Patterson."

"Chloe," Larissa said, acknowledging her with a slight incline of her head. Her only acknowledgment of Jane and Molly was the barest glance in their direction. "We'll talk later, Simon," she said curtly. Then, without another word, she walked away, forcing Gino to shepherd the others after her.

Chloe couldn't think of a thing to say.

Simon sighed. "I'm sorry about that," he said. "My mother and I had a bit of a nasty confrontation today, and I'm afraid she's still angry with me." He didn't mention Meredith's mother's presence, but there was something close to pity in his eyes.

Chloe just looked at him. Once again, she raised her chin. She didn't want his or anyone else's pity. "You don't have to be polite, Simon. We all know how your mother feels about me."

"Her behavior has nothing to do with you. Trust me. It wouldn't have mattered *who* I was dining with tonight. She's furious with me."

"Maybe so. But I'm probably her least favorite person in the world, and it can't have helped seeing you here with us."

"She'll just have to get over it."

Molly snorted. "Maybe someone needs to tell her—" she began.

Chloe kicked her under the table, and she abruptly stopped in midsentence. What point was there in saying anything else? Chloe knew Simon's mother wasn't likely to *get over it,* as he'd put it. The dislike in Larissa's eyes had been there for all the world to see. Moreover, her failure to acknowledge Chloe's introduction of Jane and Molly had made it abundantly clear that she couldn't be bothered to show even minimal courtesy to them.

Poor Simon, Chloe thought.

But poor Simon didn't seem to care that his mother was probably shooting daggers his way. Chloe couldn't actually see her because Gino had seated them in an alcove toward the back of the room, but she could imagine. Yet Simon kept casually eating and talking to Molly and Jane and acting as if nothing at all was wrong. He pretended he didn't realize Molly was still steaming mad.

Well, if he can pretend, I can, too. After all, Larissa is not my mother, nor will she be my mother-in-law. And that's the best thing to come out of this whole miserable mess.

Still, she was glad she wasn't in Simon's shoes. She'd bet he would be treated to a tirade from Larissa later tonight. And if not then it would be first thing tomorrow morning.

Under the table, Chloe laid her hand gently upon her stomach. It made her feel good to picture the tiny baby forming within. Her baby...who carried Hopewell blood...but would never know the Hopewells.

Thank God.

Chapter Five

"Well, that was certainly interesting," Jane commented as Chloe—who was driving her aunt and cousin home—pulled out of the restaurant's parking lot.

"Wasn't it," Chloe said drily.

"Actually," Molly interjected, "I'd say it was more than interesting. It was infuriating. Those Hopewells are not nice people."

"C'mon, Moll, Simon Hopewell is very nice," Chloe said.

"You thought Todd was nice, too."

Chloe winced. "He *was* nice." *Just immature. And selfish. And a few other things.*

"Why are you *defending* him?"

Chloe sighed. "I'm not. It's just that…I think it's a waste of energy to stay upset. I…need to move on."

"I'm not upset. I'm angry. Just because those snobs have a lot of money doesn't mean they can treat people like serfs."

Chloe laughed. Molly never *had* been able to hide her emotions. "And tonight you made no secret of the fact you're angry."

"So what? Let them see how it feels to have someone treat them like second-class citizens."

"Simon has never done that," Chloe said. "And remember, he gave me that check. And he certainly didn't have to."

"I still think you should have kept that check," Molly said stubbornly.

"I couldn't." Chloe would never take another thing from the Hopewells.

"Chloe did the right thing giving it back," Jane said. "But I agree with her that Simon is a nice man." She was silent for a moment, then added, "Too bad you weren't engaged to *him,* Chloe. Despite what my daughter thinks, I liked him. He's a gentleman."

As Chloe approached the main road leading to her aunt's house, she put her right turn signal on. "I wonder if Larissa Hopewell knew about that check."

"I would like to think she did," Jane said.

"God, she's a bitch," Molly said.

Chloe couldn't help but laugh. The light changed, and her lane began to move. "Notice how she never even acknowledged you when I introduced her."

"I *know!* I couldn't believe it. It's the rudest thing I've ever seen anyone do. And she pretends to be so refined. Refined, my foot."

"I personally think Larissa Hopewell is a very unhappy woman," Jane said.

"I know she makes lots of *other* people unhappy," Chloe said.

"There's usually a reason when people act that way," Jane continued thoughtfully. "Apparently she's not as upper-crust as she'd like people to believe."

"What makes you say that?"

"When I did that research on the Hopewell family, I discovered that Larissa comes from a blue-collar background. Her father worked in the steel mills, somewhere in the Cleveland area."

Chloe's mouth dropped open. "So where does she get off acting so snooty, then?"

"I'd guess it's a defense mechanism," Jane said. "If she pretends to be someone important, someone who grew up in the same social class as the Hopewell family, then it will be true."

Chloe shook her head. "So she's ashamed of her background. You know, I feel sorry for people like her. People who think money is everything."

"Maybe there's more to it than that," Jane said. "Maybe she was made to feel inferior or something. You know, by other girls. That happens a lot in high schools. Especially if she lived in a small town. You've got to be a really strong person not to let that kind of thing affect you."

"I thought you said she lived in Cleveland."

"I'm not sure where it was. Just somewhere in that area."

"Oh, Aunt Jane, you're too nice," Chloe said. "You always find an excuse for people's bad behavior."

The conversation came to a close then, as Chloe had just turned onto Maple Street and within seconds was pulling into the driveway at her aunt's house. Molly and Chloe discussed the possibility of a movie on Sunday afternoon, then the women kissed goodnight. Before leaving, Chloe promised to give her cousin a call.

As she drove the short distance to her townhouse, Chloe continued to think about Larissa Hopewell. She grimaced, remembering her aunt's defense of the woman. Chloe agreed with Molly. Her almost-mother-in-law wasn't a nice person, and now that Chloe was no longer engaged to marry Todd, she could admit it. She didn't have to kowtow to Larissa…or anyone, she thought staunchly.

There was no pretense about Simon, though. And to be fair, Todd hadn't put on airs, either. Of course, the brothers really had no need to. They'd been born into money and privilege.

Just as her unborn child would also be…if she made her pregnancy public. If it became known her child was a Hopewell.

Was she doing the right thing, keeping her child from receiving the benefits of the Hopewell name? Oh, God, why was she even thinking about this? There was no changing her decision. She'd made it, and she was standing by it, no matter what. When her baby was born, he or she would be a Patterson. And no one except for Molly and Jane would ever know her secret.

* * *

Simon was furious with his mother. He couldn't believe how rude she'd acted toward Chloe and her family. There was no excuse for her behavior. What was *wrong* with her, anyway? Chloe wouldn't hurt the Hopewells; she'd already demonstrated that. It simply wasn't in her DNA to be vindictive.

So being polite to her son's former fiancée wouldn't hurt Larissa. In fact, he'd bet the women who were with his mother tonight would have thought a lot more of her if she'd been nice to Chloe. Especially Margaret Barnes, who was the wife of the minister of the Methodist church where the Hopewells had attended for years. Margaret happened to be one of Simon's favorite people, and she was nothing if not kind.

He wondered if Liz Whitney and Blythe Belson had realized who Chloe was. At least Mrs. Belson must have. As one of his mother's circle, she had probably been treated to a few choice words about Chloe. Then again, maybe not. Maybe his mother had pretended to be—if not happy about Todd's choice in Chloe—at least not angry. Especially since appearances were so important to Larissa.

He also wondered if his mother's behavior tonight had more to do with the fact he was sitting with the Pattersons or if it was a holdover from her fury at the board meeting the day before. Either way, the rules of common courtesy demanded she be polite.

Tomorrow morning, first thing, he intended to call her and let her know exactly what he thought of her behavior tonight. In fact, he might actually call—

The insistent buzz of his cell phone cut off his thought. Picking it up he saw that there would be no need to call his mother. She was calling him. If Simon had been on the highway, he would have let the call go to voice mail. Since he was on a side street only blocks from his house, he pulled over to the curb and answered the call.

"Will you please explain to me why you were dining with *that woman?*"

"Hello to you, too, Mother," he said mildly, although he was seething.

"Answer me, Simon."

"Why shouldn't I dine with Chloe and her family?"

"You know why. It's embarrassing."

"Why is it embarrassing?"

"I wish you would stop answering my questions with a question of your own."

"If you stopped asking such stu…ridiculous questions…maybe I would answer them."

"How dare you call me stupid!"

Simon sighed. "I did not call you stupid, Mother. You're twisting my words."

"You started to."

"As a matter of fact, I didn't. I started to call your questions stupid but thought better of it." Yet they *were* stupid. Worse, they were insulting. "Okay. I'll answer your question. I was sitting with the Pattersons because they invited me to join them. And I thoroughly enjoyed having dinner with them. They're very nice people."

"Very nice people! I don't understand you, Simon. That woman has been trying to ingratiate herself into our family ever since she first met Todd. Thank goodness he finally had sense enough to realize she was all wrong for him, and trust me, we're well rid of her. Yet you persist in keeping the connection going. Next thing I know, she'll be trying to get her hooks into *you!*"

I should be so lucky. "For your information, Mother, Chloe Patterson is moving away from Riverton. So she won't be *trying to get her hooks into anyone here.*"

This information must have shocked his mother because dead silence reigned for a long moment.

"How do you know that?" she finally asked.

"She told me."

"And you believed her," his mother scoffed.

"I have no reason not to believe her. Besides, her aunt corroborated it tonight. Neither she nor her daughter are happy about her moving away, but Chloe said she won't change her mind. Now…does *that* make you happy?"

"Yes, as a matter of fact, it does. Her leaving Riverton will be best for all concerned."

Simon rolled his eyes. Man, his mother was a piece of work. "Look, I'm tired. I've had a long day."

"I'm sure it was a miserable day. I can just imagine how your news went over with the managers."

"Mother, let's not start on that. I have a headache, and I want to get home."

"You wouldn't *have* a headache if you hadn't—"

But Simon didn't hear what else she might have said, because he broke the connection and turned off his phone. And when he got home, he turned the ringer off his landline.

He'd had enough of his mother in the past two days.

* * *

Chloe awakened before five—long before her alarm, which was set for six-thirty, went off. For a few minutes, she continued to lie there. But Samson, always on high alert when it was anywhere near his feeding time, uncurled himself and silently padded up the bed until he reached her head, which he promptly began to nudge with his nose.

"Stop it." Chloe pulled her pillow out and put it over her head.

Undeterred, Samson stuck his head underneath, too, and continued to poke at her.

"Ouch," she said as he accidentally pulled at a strand of her hair. She swatted at him, but a second later, he was back. "Oh, all right," Chloe grumbled, half laughing. She tossed off the sheet and swung her legs out of bed. "If I didn't have so much to do today, I wouldn't be so agreeable," she said in a mock-disgruntled tone, which didn't fool Samson for a second.

Ten minutes later, face washed, hair brushed and pulled into a neat ponytail, lightweight cotton robe belted over her pajamas, Chloe headed downstairs where she immediately turned on the coffeemaker. Normally, coffee would be ready when she got up, because she set the timer to coincide with her alarm.

Soon the tantalizing aroma of brewing coffee filled the small kitchen, and Samson was contentedly eating. Once the coffee was ready, Chloe poured herself a mugful, added powdered creamer and a packet of Splenda and carried it out back to her small walled patio.

This was her favorite place in the mornings. Potted

plants and flowers ringed the top of the brick walls, brass wind chimes hung from the slatted wooden roof and tinkled softly in the early-morning breeze and there were even a few birds singing in nearby trees. Soon it would be light.

Chloe sat in one of the two Adirondack chairs flanking a small wrought-iron table and sipped her coffee. The weather was cool—probably too cool to be sitting outside—but Chloe didn't mind. After a long winter filled with snow and freezing temperatures, she was so glad to see the approach of summer; she didn't care if it was sixty or ninety out. She'd take what she could get and enjoy it.

For a while, she thought about her day. She had promised a client she'd have a new design for her to view no later than three o'clock, and she also wanted to get started going through her closets. And she needed to make a trip to the supermarket. She was nearly out of milk and coffee. She made a mental note to look through the pantry and fridge and see what else she might be low on.

And don't forget that Simon is coming by to pick up Todd's things.

She smiled wryly. As if she could forget. In fact, she found it alarming how often thoughts of Simon came to mind. She didn't understand *why* they did. For someone who was supposedly in love with his brother less than two weeks ago, she sure was spending a lot of time thinking about Simon instead.

So don't think about him, then. Get up and get busy. He has no business being in your thoughts, and you know it.

She drained her mug, then stood and walked inside where she put an English muffin in the toaster and poured herself more coffee.

By seven, breakfast eaten, showered and dressed, she was hard at work on the promised design for her client. By nine, the design had reached the point where she could e-mail it to her client to see if she was on the right track. Once that was accomplished, Chloe stretched and decided to make herself a cup of tea.

She had just put a mug of water into the microwave when the phone rang. Her caller ID showed it was Simon Hopewell. Despite her minilecture to herself earlier, a little frisson of excitement rippled through her.

"Would it be convenient if I came by in about thirty minutes?" he asked.

"Sure."

"Okay. See you then."

She stood looking at the phone for long moments after the call was disconnected. She had no idea why she felt so unsettled.

Eventually, she walked upstairs and carefully made one last check of the bedroom and bathroom to make sure she hadn't overlooked any of Todd's belongings. Discovering a package of razor blades hidden behind some face cream in the bathroom cabinet, she tossed them into the shopping bag where she'd packed everything else and took it downstairs where she put it on the bottom step.

She eyed the powder room under the stairwell, and after a small argument with herself, she walked in and checked her hair in the mirror. She didn't like what she saw. Her hair needed brushing, and she had no lipstick on. Telling herself that she didn't ever want any Hopewell to see her looking less than her best, she raced back upstairs. While there, she decided to change into a nicer outfit than her standard work uniform of loose cotton pants and an oversize T-shirt, so she hurriedly put on a pair of khaki shorts, a fitted pink striped tee and matching pink flip-flops. Finally, she powdered her nose and put on some mascara, too. When she was done, she inspected herself to make sure she hadn't overdone the makeup. Nope. She looked fine. In fact, she looked darned good. *Take that, Todd Hopewell.* But even as the thought formed, she knew Todd had nothing to do with her primping.

Not able to concentrate on work now that Simon was on his way, she busied herself with making her grocery list while watching the clock. She didn't have long to wait. Almost exactly thirty minutes after Simon's call, Chloe's doorbell rang. She checked the peephole to make sure it was him, then opened the door.

"Good morning." He gave her a friendly smile.

He had the nicest eyes. She'd never imagined gray eyes could seem warm, but his did. Maybe it was because when he smiled, he smiled with his eyes, too, and you knew he meant it—that he wasn't just being polite. "Good morning," she said.

Today he was dressed casually—in khaki shorts and a dark blue knit shirt. His legs were long and muscular—athletic legs. She remembered that Todd had once said Simon played soccer in college, whereas he, Todd, had preferred football.

Standing aside so Simon could enter, she caught a whiff of some kind of woodsy cologne or aftershave. It had a nice, clean smell—the kind she liked best.

He smiled at her. His glance took in her legs, too, she noticed. Chloe considered her legs her best feature, and she was suddenly glad she'd showcased them in shorts and that she'd had a recent pedicure.

"I, um…those are Todd's things sitting on the step. In that bag."

His smile faded a bit. "Oh. Okay."

God, she was being rude. She should have asked him if he'd like some coffee or something.

But he hadn't moved. Instead, he looked at her, his expression turning thoughtful. "Listen, Chloe, I, uh, want to apologize for my mother's behavior last night."

Chloe flushed and tried to cover her embarrassment with a shrug. "Don't worry about it."

"But I *did* worry about it." His eyes hardened. "I'm tired of my family acting badly. Between Todd and my mother, I'm not sure who's worse. You must be sick of all of us."

Chloe swallowed. She didn't want to talk about Todd *or* his mother. "It…" She took a deep breath. "It's not up to you to apologize for either one of them. You're not responsible for their actions."

"Maybe not, but there was simply no excuse for last night. I can imagine what your aunt and cousin must think."

Chloe shrugged again. "Aunt Jane wasn't upset." She refused to lie and say Molly wasn't upset, though. Besides, he knew better.

"She's a better person than I am, then. In her shoes, I'd have wanted to smack my mother."

Chloe couldn't help smiling at the image his words conjured. Wouldn't *that* have been something to see?

"See? You feel the same way," he said, smiling now himself.

"Let's not talk about it anymore. It's over and done with." *And I probably will never see Larissa Hopewell again.* Feeling really awkward now, she hesitated for a moment, then said, "Um, would you like a cup of coffee or something?"

He glanced at his watch. "I'd better not. I've got a tee time of eleven-thirty."

"Oh, I'm keeping you, then."

"No, I've got plenty of time to get to the club—just not enough to sit over coffee." Walking to the steps, he picked up the shopping bag. "You've got a lot to do today, too, I'm sure."

"Well…yes, I…want to get started going through my things. See what I might want to throw out before I begin packing." She inclined her head toward the stack of boxes that had been sitting in the hallway for weeks—ever since she and Todd had decided that after they were married it made more sense for her to leave her rented townhome than for him to sell his condo.

Simon frowned. "You're not leaving *that* soon. To begin packing now, I mean."

"No, but no sense leaving everything to the last minute."

He nodded. "That's probably smart. Well, I guess I'll be on my way, then."

"Thanks for coming by." She opened the door again.

"You're welcome."

She waited for him to move past her. She had no idea what to say. Nice to have known you? Hope you have a nice life? Tell that brother of yours he's a first-class bastard?

He broke the silence. "I hope we'll see each other again before you leave Riverton."

"I hope so, too."

"Maybe...I could take you to dinner one night before you go."

Chloe was surprised by how much she'd have liked to say yes. "That's really nice of you, Simon, but it's not necessary." She smiled to soften her words. "Besides, you *did* take me to dinner last night." She still felt funny about allowing him to pick up the check for all of them, even though she knew he certainly could afford it.

"That hardly counts."

"Of course, it counts."

"How about this," he said. "I'll call you. Maybe you'll change your mind."

Before she could answer, he waved, then headed for his car—a black Lexus he'd parked out front.

Chloe didn't wait for him to get in and pull away. Instead, she shut the door and leaned back against it. As she had so often in the past weeks, she touched her stomach. It was still almost as flat as it ever had been, but she knew it would begin to change soon. *Would he have been wanting to see me again if he knew what I'm hiding?* Without warning, tears filled her eyes, and an overwhelming sadness flooded her.

I'm scared.

She'd been denying it—to herself, to her aunt, to Molly. But she could no longer pretend—not to herself, anyway. She was scared. Really, really scared.

No matter how much she talked to herself, no matter how many times she told herself she was better off without Todd, that she was perfectly capable of having this baby and raising it herself, she knew her future wasn't going to be a walk in the park.

No wonder she was scared.

She'd have to be an idiot not to be.

Simon hadn't wanted to leave Chloe this morning. In fact, he'd almost blown off his golf game and accepted her offer of coffee. As much as he'd thought he wanted nothing more than to enjoy a relaxing Saturday on the golf course, he knew now he'd much rather have figured out some way to spend the day with Chloe.

The admission bothered the hell out of him.

Are you nuts? Chloe is your brother's ex-fiancée. Your mother detests her. Even if she was staying in Riverton, any kind of relationship with her would be impossible. She is off-limits. How many times do you have to tell yourself this? Put her out of your mind!

Yet for the rest of the day, all the while he was playing golf and exchanging pleasantries with the rest of his foursome, Chloe remained stubbornly lodged on the periphery of his thoughts.

He just hoped this wasn't a permanent problem.

Because there didn't seem to be a damn thing he could do about it.

Chapter Six

Simon called Chloe on Monday, and his call went straight to voice mail. He left a message saying he'd hoped she might have changed her mind about letting him take her to dinner. He gave her his cell-phone number and said to call him if she was free either Wednesday or Thursday night. He figured she might be more inclined to accept his dinner invitation if he didn't suggest seeing her on a weekend.

She didn't call him back.

He told himself that was that. To forget about her.

Yet he couldn't seem to get her out of his mind. It was driving him crazy. "Dammit, I want to see her," he muttered. "If only to make sure she's okay."

Yeah, right, that's the reason. Just to make sure

she's okay. That's why she's occupying most of your waking thoughts.

Okay, so he liked Chloe. Maybe even more than liked her. And she liked him. He was sure of it. In fact, he'd swear she'd wanted to say yes when he'd suggested dinner on Saturday. Yet she'd said no.

All right, so he had a problem. But he'd come up against tough situations before and figured out a way to solve them. Surely he could come up with some legitimate reason to call her, some perfectly logical reason he had to see her that had nothing to do with taking her to dinner, something she wouldn't be able to refuse.

Finally, on Thursday afternoon, he had a brainstorm. If she shot down his idea, well, then he'd go to plan B. What plan B might be he had no clue. He'd figure that out when and if he had to.

Getting up from his desk, he walked to the doorway that separated his office from Maggie's. He saw she was engrossed in a PowerPoint presentation that he would be using at tomorrow's manager's meeting. After clearing his throat to alert her to his presence, he said, "Maggie, take messages for a while, will you? I've got a phone call to make."

She barely looked up. "Hmm? Oh, sure, Simon."

He smiled at her distracted answer. When she was working on something, Maggie was completely focused. He'd often teased her, saying if the building was on fire and she was in the middle of something she considered important, the fire would just have to wait.

Still amused, he closed the door behind him as he walked back into his office. A moment later, he picked up the phone. Since he was going to present Chloe with a business proposition, this time instead of calling her home phone he would call her cell, which was what was listed on her business card.

She answered on the third ring. "Chloe Patterson."

"Chloe, it's Simon Hopewell."

"Hello, Simon."

"I was wondering if you had any time tomorrow or Saturday when we could get together. I want to talk to you about something."

For a long moment, she said nothing. Just when Simon thought she wasn't going to answer, she said, "Look, I just don't think it's a good idea."

Knowing instinctively it wouldn't be smart to play dumb, he said, "I understand why you might feel that way, but I have some business I'd like to discuss with you."

"What kind of business?" She didn't try to disguise the skepticism in her voice.

"A completely new Web site for the company."

"What?" Now her voice was filled with incredulity. "Why? More to the point, why would you want to talk to *me* about it?"

"Have you ever looked at our Web site?"

"Yes, actually, I have."

"Then you know it's hopelessly pedestrian. No sex appeal at all."

"Sex appeal? You want sex appeal?"

"Don't laugh. Every company needs sex appeal nowadays, even companies like ours that manufacture sexless industrial equipment. In fact," he added, warming up to the subject, "we probably need it more than any other kind of company."

"Simon, I doubt any of your prospective customers care a thing about what kind of Web site you have."

"A dynamic Web presence is a necessity in the new global marketplace, Chloe. I would think you'd be one of the first to realize this."

More silence. Then, "Are you serious, Simon? You really want a new Web site?"

"Deadly serious."

"Okay, fine. Now answer my other question. Why me?"

"Why not you?"

"I'm hardly a big-time designer. In fact, I've built my entire business around designing and maintaining Web sites for the little guy."

"Then it's time you stopped being prejudiced against big companies and took on someone like Hopewell. I promise you this won't be a walk in the park because I'm told I'm stubborn and demanding, but it'll be worth it to you financially."

"I *knew* that's what this was about."

"What's that supposed to mean?"

"Oh, come *on,* Simon. We both know what it means."

"Chloe, will you at least talk to me about doing the work?"

"That's really not a good idea."

"Now it's my turn to ask why not?"

"I've already told you why not. I have no experience with your type of business or with such a big job. I think you'd be better off to—"

"I'm not going to take no for an answer," he interrupted. "I just want to discuss the possibility. I trust you, and I'd like to see what you think about my ideas. I'll tell you what. I'll make a deal with you. If after we talk you think you can't handle it, then I'll look elsewhere. But you'll have to help me find someone else I can trust." He crossed his fingers mentally, counting on the fact he already knew she wasn't the kind of person to back down from a challenge.

She sighed audibly. "All right, fine. But I can't spare any time tomorrow. I'm working like crazy trying to finish a job for a client who's giving me fits. It's running late because she kept changing her mind, so now she's in a frenzy. Anyway, to get her off my back, I promised her the site would go live tomorrow afternoon. Otherwise she'd be bombarding me with calls, e-mails and text messages. Honestly, sometimes you just have to laugh or you'd scream. Or commit murder." She made an exasperated sound. "Sorry for the rant."

He grinned. He liked that she had a temper. People who couldn't get mad when it was a reasonable reaction were boring. "That's okay. You ought to hear me around here some days."

"I should have time to meet on Saturday, though. Is morning okay?"

"I'd prefer afternoon. Can we make it, say, four, four-thirty?" He figured he could string the meeting out until at least six and then, if he was lucky, persuade her to have dinner with him.

"Four-thirty's fine. Where do you want to meet? There or here?"

"I'll come there."

He smiled in satisfaction as they said goodbye. Plan A was going to work. He could feel it in his bones.

Chloe had the devil of a time getting her concentration back after the phone call from Simon. This whole him-wanting-her-to-design-the-company's-new-Web-site thing had to be a ploy to get her to take the five thousand dollars he'd tried to give her before. No matter what he said, he wasn't fooling her. He supposedly wanted her help, but his ultimate intent was to assuage his conscience about the treatment she'd received from his family. There was no other explanation for it. Because even a fool could see—and she wasn't a fool—that even if he really *did* want a new Web site for the company, he could afford to hire the very best in Web designers, the sort of big-time professionals who normally worked with large, multinational corporate clients. Her biggest customer so far was a local supermarket. The others were mostly all small business owners.

Chloe wasn't complaining. She knew she'd been lucky; she'd carved out a niche—well, two of them, actually. Her first break came when a college friend became an innovative wedding photographer based in southern California who asked her to design his Web site. As his work gained status and he began speaking at conferences and giving workshops, other photographers checked out his site, liked what they saw, then started calling her. Now she had close to two dozen photography sites, many of which she maintained on a monthly basis, and the list kept growing.

The same thing had happened with the bed-and-breakfast business. Several years ago, she and Molly had taken a vacation to the Door County area of Wisconsin. They'd stayed in a bed-and-breakfast and become friendly with the owner, a young woman only a few years older than they were. When the owner, Beth, found out what Chloe did for a living, she asked her to do a Web site for her. From there, Chloe's stable of bed-and-breakfast sites grew to more than thirty, with new ones being added every couple of months.

Chloe knew she was good, but she wasn't in the same league as the big-name designers, mainly because she didn't have the resources they did. But that was okay with her. She liked the size of her business. It was perfect for her, bringing in a decent income, yet leaving her enough free time to have a life.

If she took on a corporate client like Hopewell Enterprises, she would no longer be able to handle the business herself. She'd have to hire an assistant. Just the thought of bringing someone into her home or having to lease office space to accommodate another employee alarmed her. She liked her low overhead, her freedom....

And yet...there was a part of her that was itching to show Simon *and* Todd...and especially Larissa that she, Chloe, could do something they couldn't do. Something valuable.

Damn Simon. Dangling this carrot. Tempting me not just with this work but with the possibility of working with him.

Yes, there was that, too. The fact that if she took this job, she would need to see and talk with Simon. Often.

Even the thought of saying yes frightened her.

It's too dangerous. Don't forget you're pregnant.
With a Hopewell baby! If you're around Simon too
much, he might suspect. And what about afterward?
What if he wants you to not only design the Web site but
maintain it, too? He'd have to come to Syracuse or
you'd have to come back to Riverton periodically.

Oh, God, why had she agreed to talk to him? She
should have just said no to begin with. Seeing him,
knowing how persuasive he could be, was just asking
for trouble.

She took a deep breath, told herself to settle down.
She didn't *have* to agree to do the work. All she'd committed to was a meeting. He couldn't *make* her agree to
anything she didn't want to do.

All she had to do on Saturday was listen then politely
decline. And if he argued she would say that as flattered
as she was by his interest in her work that she simply
didn't have the time to take on a job of this magnitude.
Yes. That was the sensible thing to do. Spending that kind
of time with Simon Hopewell, no matter how tempting,
was simply too dangerous to her peace of mind. And to
her plans for the future. *And your baby's future!*

End of story.

So why, then, if she'd made her decision, did she still
feel so uneasy about Saturday's meeting?

Simon pulled up in front of Chloe's townhouse at
exactly four-twenty-five on Saturday. He didn't immediately get out of the car. Instead, he took a couple of
minutes to make sure he had all his arguments lined up,
because he was certain Chloe would have spent the time

between his phone call Thursday and his visit today to line up her *own* arguments as to why she couldn't do the new Web site design.

Simon wondered what his colleagues would think when they discovered what he'd done. Especially since he planned to pay for a new Web site out of his own personal funds. He knew Mark, in particular, would wonder if he'd lost his mind. Who paid for something like this out of their own pocket? Who authorized a major redo of their company's Web site without consulting their marketing and PR departments? Certainly Simon wasn't that kind of CEO. He still hadn't figured out how he'd explain his actions when his colleagues *did* find out about them, but he'd cross that bridge when he came to it.

Right now his first priority was getting Chloe to agree to do the work. Glancing at her unit, he saw slight movement through the big front window. Thinking maybe she'd looked out and seen him sitting in the car, he grabbed his briefcase containing all the material he wanted to give her and got out of the car.

Because this was a business meeting, Simon wore pressed slacks with an open-at-the-throat pale gray cotton shirt and polished loafers. He was setting the tone, he thought in amusement.

She opened the front door before he'd reached the stoop. Her smile seemed genuine as she greeted him. Holding the door wide, she said, "C'mon in. Otherwise Samson may decide to make a dash for freedom. He continues to think he might like it better outside." She made a face. "He doesn't realize he has no front claws."

"Some of us don't."

This brought a burst of laughter from her. He liked hearing her laugh. *Who are you kidding? You like everything about her.* He especially liked the way she looked today in what he imagined was her work uniform—jeans that showed off her curves, clogs and a couple of sleeveless, layered T-shirts, one green, one white. Her arms had nice muscle tone, he noticed. He wondered if she worked out. She must. She wouldn't look as good as she did—especially with her sedentary job—if she didn't hit the gym.

"I thought we could sit outside on the patio," she said. "It's such a nice day, and I've been cooped up most of it, unfortunately."

"That's great with me. I spent too much time inside myself."

"How about something to drink while we talk? Iced tea, maybe? Or would you rather have a beer?"

"Since this is business, let's make it tea." Later he would buy a bottle of wine they could share over dinner. Even the thought gave him a pleasant stirring of anticipation.

She wended her way around the moving supplies that were stacked in the hallway and beckoned him to follow. At the back of the unit there was a small, sun-filled kitchen decorated in soft yellow with red accents. A cheerful kitchen, he thought, comparing it to his own white, utilitarian one that he rarely used. He liked hers a lot better. Looking around, he spied her cat, who sat squarely in the middle of a rag rug in front of the back door. His green eyes stared unblinkingly at Simon. Simon had never really liked cats. He was more a dog person, but this little guy seemed cool.

"Samson must like you," Chloe said as she lifted a pitcher of tea from the refrigerator.

"How do you know?"

"Easy. He didn't take off."

And how do you feel about me? For one alarming moment, Simon feared he'd expressed the thought aloud.

"What?" she said, frowning.

"That's me," Simon said lightly. "Loved by kids and animals."

"Don't make a face. That's actually a high recommendation, you know. Kids and animals seem to know instinctively who the good guys are." She set the pitcher on the counter and took two tall glasses out of the cabinet above.

The thought crossed Simon's mind that his mother, for all her faults, had a number of good qualities—probably more than Chloe would ever believe, because the family dog certainly loved Larissa. So had all the dogs they'd had over the years, even though technically they'd been his father's dogs. His mother could also be generous when she wanted to be. Even though she did nothing but complain about Noah's vocation, she contributed liberally to Riverton's homeless shelter, as well as the local library. In fact, she was probably the library's biggest donor. She didn't toot her own horn, either, or seek recognition for her generosity. Trouble was, his mother was a study in contradictions. Just when Simon thought he understood her, just when she exasperated him most, she would surprise him by doing something totally unexpected and opposite to his perception of her character.

By now Simon and Chloe had walked out to a pleasant brick-walled patio, and the cat slipped out with them. "You allow him out?" Simon asked.

"He can't climb the wall or jump that high," she said. "So yes, he comes out here with me all the time. Once in a while, if he's lucky, he'll catch a bug or two." She laughed. "It can be frustrating for him, though, because he'd love to get the birds. There's one particular mockingbird who lives to torment him, staying just out of his reach but close enough to lure Samson into thinking he can leap up and get him. It's actually quite funny to watch." Her tone softened, and she leaned down to pet the cat. "Poor Sammy. I shouldn't make fun of you."

Simon never thought he'd be envious of a cat, but he wouldn't mind having her pet *him*. The cat wasn't the only frustrated being out here today, he thought ruefully. Chloe's closeness tantalized him. Right now he could smell the light fragrance she wore mixed with the lemony scent of her shampoo. Too bad he couldn't do a whole lot about it. At least not what he wanted to do.

"Shall we get started?" She seemed oblivious to his inner turmoil.

They sat across from each other with a small wrought-iron table between them. Simon unloaded his briefcase and handed her a wish list he'd prepared.

For the next hour, he answered her questions and elaborated on what he thought should be done to change the existing Hopewell Web site. Winding up, he said, "I thought we might spend some time looking at some of our competitors' Web sites, and I could tell you what I like about them and what I dislike."

She looked away and appeared to be considering his suggestion. The afternoon sunlight, filtered through the slatted roof overhead, gave her hair honeyed highlights.

"What are you thinking?" he prodded. "Do I want the impossible?"

She shook her head and turned to meet his gaze. "No, that's not it. The problem is, much as I'd enjoy the challenge of working on a new Web site for the company, I don't have the time to take on such a large project, Simon. I'm already fully booked for at least the next six months."

"Really," he said flatly.

"Yes, really." But her gaze dropped, and she once again bent to stroke her cat.

"C'mon, Chloe. You can be honest with me. I *know* that's not true."

"But it *is* true."

"If it's so true, why won't you look at me?"

For a long moment, she didn't answer. Nor did she look up to meet his gaze. It was very quiet, the only sounds the plop, plop, plop of water from a nearby fountain and the muted roar of a jet flying high overhead.

"If you were fully booked *for the next six months,* how would you have managed both a wedding and a honeymoon?"

Finally she looked at him. In her green eyes he saw a combination of emotions, all but one of which he couldn't identify. "All right, I exaggerated. I'm not fully booked for six months. But I do have too much on my plate. The move. My existing clients. Some proposals already out to various prospective clients, several of which I know will want me to do their work. Plus there's a workshop for some new design software that's going to be offered after the holidays, and I'd love to take it. I've got other commitments in January, as well. So you see? I really don't have time to take on something like the Hopewell Web site."

Damn. What she'd said had the ring of truth.

"I'm sorry, Simon. Under other circumstances I would have enjoyed working with you."

That, too, held the ring of truth.

"I'm sorry, too," he said. "I think you would have done a great job for us." He began to gather up his papers. Casually, he glanced at his watch. "I wondered why my stomach was growling. It's nearly six, and I didn't have any lunch." Before she could comment, he added, "Since you turned me down on the Web site, I think the least you can do is come and have some dinner with me."

She started to shake her head.

"Don't say no. I hate eating alone."

Her lovely eyes filled with genuine regret. "I really can't, Simon. I already have plans for the evening."

Hell. Was she already dating? Is that why she hadn't called him back on Monday? Even the thought made him clench his teeth.

In that case, he guessed he'd better start thinking. Because it looked as if he'd have to go to plan B.

And fast.

Chapter Seven

"Why didn't you tell Simon where you were going tonight?" Molly asked after Chloe filled her in on his visit.

"Honestly? I don't know." Chloe had been thinking about this very thing ever since Simon had left her place earlier.

Molly lowered the sound on the Sarah Brightman CD. "You know what I think?"

Chloe laughed. "You'll tell me whether I want to know or not, won't you?"

Molly grinned. Without taking her eyes off the unfamiliar street or losing her concentration—they were on their way to a baby shower being given for a mutual friend, and Molly couldn't remember exactly which house the hostess lived in—she said, "I think you're playing with fire, *that's* what I think."

"I don't know what you mean."

"Oh, Chloe, come *on!* This is me you're talking to. Don't play dumb."

Chloe eyed her cousin. Sometimes she wished Molly didn't know her so well. "It's none of Simon's business what I'm doing or where I'm going."

"That's not the point. Dang! That was the house." Molly hit the brakes. "The point is, you didn't *not* tell Simon you were going to a baby shower tonight because you wanted him to think you had a date."

"So what?"

Molly managed a U-turn and drove back to the house where the shower was taking place. There were several cars parked nearby. "We're early. Want to sit out here for a while?"

"I don't care."

Molly pressed the power button on her Prius and set the emergency brake. "If I thought you wanted Simon to think you had a date because he would tell Todd, which would let that jerk know you're not sitting around crying over him, then I'd be giving you the thumbs-up. But what worries me is you did what you did because subconsciously you wanted to make Simon jealous."

"That's *not* true."

But Chloe couldn't help wondering if Molly was right. *Was* that the real reason she'd kept quiet earlier? If so, she was skidding into really dangerous territory.

"The one thing you did right was turn down his offer, but I think you should avoid any more contact with him."

"I'd already decided that. Even before he came over."

"Then why did you see him today?"

"I couldn't get out of it. He's very persuasive."

"He's a Hopewell," Molly said. "He's not used to being told no."

Chloe stared at her. "You still don't like him, do you?"

Molly shrugged. "It's not that I don't like him. It's that I don't trust him. Not entirely. I mean, come on. The man had you *investigated,* for crying out loud."

"But he explained—"

"I don't care what bull honky excuse he gave you!" Molly's eyes glittered dangerously. "That was a really crappy thing to do, and you know it."

"Nobody's perfect, Moll. Not even you."

Molly opened her mouth. Shut it. Blew out a breath. "I guess I deserved that. It's just that…I don't want to see you get hurt again. And I can't see how any ongoing relationship with Simon Hopewell could ever result in anything good."

Chloe reached over and squeezed her cousin's hand. "I know you're only thinking of me," she said softly. "But I'm a big girl. I can take care of myself."

"But, Chloe—" breaking off abruptly, she made a face "—oh, shoot. I'll stop. I've said my piece. You know how I feel. It's your life."

Chloe smiled. She reached for the wrapped presents in the backseat. "Aunt Jane likes Simon a lot." She handed Molly hers.

"Mom isn't always right, you know."

"Maybe not always but most of the time she is. I respect her opinion."

"I do, too, and if you weren't pregnant, Chloe, I wouldn't think a thing of you flirting with Simon and even dating him if you wanted to. Although why you'd want to have anything to do with any of the Hopewells is beyond me."

Chloe started to laugh. "I thought you said you were through lecturing me."

"I'm just saying." And then Molly began to laugh, too. "Oh, let's go inside. I think it's time."

A cute redhead opened the door. "Hi," she said with a wide smile that revealed dimples on both cheeks. "Carol's in the kitchen, so I'm the official greeter right now. I'm Reese Belson. C'mon in."

Reese Belson! Chloe hoped her smile didn't reveal how rattled she felt by coming face-to-face with Meredith's younger sister.

"Hi," Molly said in her cheery teacher voice. "I'm Molly Patterson, and this is my cousin Chloe."

Reese's eyes widened almost imperceptibly, but whatever she was feeling was quickly banished, and her smile didn't falter. Chloe, on the other hand, wished she could turn around and go back home. She didn't need this.

But there was no way she could leave. So, along with Molly, Chloe followed Reese through a large archway that led into a long, rectangular living room that made an L-turn into an adjoining dining room. Half a dozen chattering, laughing young women were already scattered around.

"Help yourself to some champagne punch or iced tea," Reese said, pointing to the dining room. "Carol's just getting the rest of the food put out. We'll eat when everyone gets here. Oh, and I'll take your gifts. We're piling them over there by that big chair. That's where our mama-to-be will be sitting."

As Chloe handed Reese her shower gift, their eyes met. What was Meredith's sister thinking? Whatever it was, she continued to hide it well. Her hazel eyes betrayed nothing except friendliness. Determined to be as unaffected as Reese seemed to be, Chloe thanked her and kept her own smile firmly in place.

"Is that who I think it is?" Molly said sotto voce after Reese walked away.

"Yes, I'm afraid so."

"You okay?"

"I'm fine."

Molly squeezed Chloe's arm. "Good. Keep that chin up. You have nothing to be ashamed of."

Loyal Molly. *What would I do without her?* Chloe pushed aside the reminder that she would *have* to do without her soon. Because no matter what Chloe had said to her cousin and aunt about the move and how they'd still see each other a lot, the truth was that it would be very different living that far away from them. *Don't think about it. Not tonight. Just think about keeping your chin up the way Molly said.*

After getting a drink each, Chloe and Molly said hello to the other guests, some of whom Chloe already knew. Because of Reese's presence, Chloe knew she wouldn't really relax, no matter how many pep talks she gave herself. Oh, God. Did all these other women know about her engagement to Todd? They probably did. After all, the engagement had been announced in the

Riverton Record months earlier and had been accompanied by a photo of Chloe and Todd together. *I guess the real question is do they know he dumped me for Meredith?* There'd been no formal announcement of the marriage yet that Chloe knew of. Still, in a town the size of Riverton they were bound to have heard some gossip. After all, it had been more than two weeks now since he'd sent Chloe that Dear Jane letter. News traveled fast in small towns. Especially news this juicy.

Was Joanne Woodson giving her an odd look? Linda Bowman and Cate Holland had certainly acted funny when Chloe said hello. Even Lisa Morrow, who was one of the sweetest people in the world, had acted strange.

"Chloe, you look great." This came from Marsha Wagner, a local floral designer, who was one of Chloe's clients.

"Thanks. So do you." What did Marsha mean by that? *Can she tell I'm pregnant?* Chloe knew she had to stop being so paranoid—no one could *possibly* know she was pregnant yet—but she couldn't seem to help herself. Tonight she felt exposed…and raw.

Every couple of minutes, the doorbell chimed and someone else arrived. By seven-thirty, there were a couple dozen young women gathered, and Carol Falco, the hostess, invited all of them to get something to eat. "Afterward, we'll play some games," she said. Several of the women moaned, and everyone laughed. Chloe joined in, but her laugh was forced. She wondered if she could plead a migraine or something. She tried to catch Molly's eye, but her cousin was in an animated conversation with a fellow teacher and didn't look up. Chloe sighed in defeat and got in line for the food. She really *was* starving. Thank goodness her pregnancy had not affected her appetite. She wasn't experiencing morning sickness, either. That nausea she'd felt a few weeks back must have been due to wedding nerves and not the pregnancy.

As the women filled their plates, Jenna Pappas, the honoree, hugely pregnant—in fact, she looked ready to pop, Chloe thought—was settled into the designated chair, and Reese, who seemed to be Carol's helper for the evening, brought her a plate of food.

"Such service," Jenna said. Her smile was bright enough to light up the entire room. *That'll be me soon, but I won't have anyone to wait on me.*

Shocking her, Chloe's eyes filled with tears. She blinked rapidly. *Stop it. Just stop it.* Why had she come? Why hadn't she realized her emotions would be in such turmoil tonight? She guessed she had figured she was doing so well she could handle anything. But she hadn't counted on how she would feel when she saw Jenna—so happy, so excited about the birth of her first baby. Jenna, who had a husband who adored her. Jenna, who would not be raising her child alone. Jenna, whose friends were all gathered around her and wishing her well.

Chloe knew she wasn't going to be able to stay. She wasn't as strong as she'd thought. Maybe she'd never been as strong as she'd thought. Walking out to the kitchen, she set her half-filled plate down on the counter. Then she wandered out into the hallway where she spied an open powder-room door. After inspecting herself in the vanity mirror to make sure the tears were gone, she took a deep breath and headed back to the living room.

"Moll," she said quietly, walking up behind her.

Molly turned around, took one look at her and without saying a word, walked out to the entryway where they would have some privacy. "What's wrong?"

"I don't feel well. Can I take your car? You can get a ride to my place afterward, can't you?"

"What do you mean, you don't feel well? Is it Reese? 'Cause I don't think—"

"Moll, please. It's a lot of things. I just know I have to get out of here. Otherwise I might have a meltdown."

Chloe knew Molly wanted to ask a million more questions. Instead, she handed Chloe her plate. "Hold this a minute." Then she walked into the living room, found her purse where she'd stashed it earlier, took out her keys and came back and handed them to Chloe. "I'll call you later…just before I leave here."

"Okay. I know I'm being a coward, but make my apologies, will you? Say I can feel a terrible migraine coming on and had to go home."

Chloe was able to hold in everything she was feeling until she'd driven out of sight of the house. Then she pulled over, put the car in Park and allowed herself to fall apart.

Simon knew he was acting like a silly kid. In fact, he couldn't believe he had just driven past Chloe's townhouse not once but twice! And now he was parked across the street—not directly across but just close enough that he could see her driveway clearly. He'd already determined she wasn't home, although there was a Prius parked in front of her unit. Still, her place was dark, at least from the front, and he sure as hell wasn't going to get out and walk around to the back to see if her car was parked in its parking slot. Someone might think he was a burglar.

This is stupid. What are you going to do if she comes home and sees you? What will she think? The good thing was that he wasn't driving his Lexus; he was in a company SUV—and he didn't think she'd recognize it, so he should be okay even if she *did* see the vehicle.

Simon looked at his watch. He pressed the button that lighted up the face. 10:15 p.m. He knew he should go home. But something simply wouldn't let him. He wanted to see if she came home alone or if someone brought her home.

Doesn't matter what you want. You have no right to spy on her, and you know it. She's not your girlfriend...and she never will be.

But no matter how much he knew what he was doing was wrong he couldn't seem to make himself move. And soon he didn't have that option because not five minutes later, a car—he thought it was a Honda but couldn't tell for sure—pulled up in back of the Prius and the passenger door opened. Simon blinked. It wasn't Chloe. It was her cousin, Molly, clearly visible in the car's inner light. *Hell!* Simon sank down in his seat, even though she wasn't looking in his direction. She stood there, bent down so she could see into the car and talked to the driver for a moment. Simon didn't know who the driver was—another female, that's all he knew.

A few seconds later, Molly closed the door and waved

at the driver. Then she walked to the front door. He couldn't see if she rang the doorbell or knocked, but a few minutes later the inside hall light went on, and the door opened. Chloe stood there.

He was lucky Molly hadn't seen him. What if she had? And what if she'd told Chloe she'd seen him sitting outside?

Would she believe he'd just needed to know if she was okay? Probably not. He guessed he'd never know for sure. What he *did* know for sure was that he'd better get a grip. He was way too old to be acting like this.

Chloe felt better the next day. She had quit berating herself for giving way to her emotions the night before. She told herself to count her blessings and stop thinking about what she *didn't* have.

Determinedly, she spent all of Sunday working through her closet and sorting out the clothes she wanted to keep and the ones she wanted to put in the church donation bag. While working, she listened to her favorite playlists on her iPod and ruthlessly kept her earphones plugged in and her thoughts as far away from the Hopewell brothers and everything concerning them—even her pregnancy—as she could.

Tomorrow she would once again reenter the real world. She had made a one o'clock appointment to see Dr. Ramsey for her first prenatal visit.

But for today Chloe wanted both her body and her mind to stay right here, in her safe cocoon, where the world couldn't touch her, and not think about anything more complicated than her wardrobe.

* * *

On Monday morning, Simon was halfway to his office when his cell phone buzzed. Seeing it was his mother, he decided to let the call go to voice mail and return it when he arrived at work. What now? he wondered. He wasn't in the mood for any kind of confrontation.

He put off even listening to her message until he'd dealt with his e-mail and looked at his calendar for the day. Even then he needed the fortification of a cup of coffee before he felt ready to deal with the call.

"I was hoping you could come for dinner tonight," she said after answering on the second ring.

At least she didn't still seem angry. That was something. "What's the occasion?" he asked, stalling. If she wanted him to come just so she could continue to berate him about money, he would have other plans.

"Todd and Meredith are home. They got in last night. I thought a little celebratory dinner with the family was in order. Noah's coming," she added, "although he's insisted on bringing someone with him. Honestly, I don't understand him sometimes."

Simon nearly choked trying to suppress a snort. *Sometimes.* That was an understatement. She had never understood Noah, although he had to admit he was surprised himself. Had Noah ever brought anyone to a family gathering before? He didn't think so. "All right. I'll be there. What time?"

"Seven for cocktails. We'll dine at eight. And Simon…I want no talk of Chloe Patterson tonight. If you have anything to say to Todd, say it privately, please."

Although Simon agreed with his mother that a dinner

that included Meredith and Noah's unknown guest was not a suitable venue for airing grievances with Todd, he prickled with irritation at her imperious tone. Yet he forced himself to say an even, "I know how to behave civilly, Mother." *Unlike someone else I could mention.* But Simon could tell she knew what he was thinking.

To her credit, his mother only said, "Thank you."

After hanging up, Simon sat thinking for a while. He almost picked up the phone again to call Noah. But he decided not to. Noah rarely had time to talk at the shelter, and Mondays seemed to be one of their busiest days. For some reason, Noah once told Simon that more of Riverton's homeless descended upon the shelter on Sundays than any other day, if only for a hot meal.

Off and on during the day, Simon's thoughts strayed to the approaching dinner. It promised to be interesting. Very interesting.

He could hardly wait.

Chapter Eight

Chloe liked the doctor Molly had recommended the moment she saw her. Dr. Ramsey looked to be in her late fifties, with blond hair and friendly brown eyes. She wore an open white lab coat over a striking brown-and-gold geometric print dress. "Hello, Chloe," she said with a welcoming smile. "I'm Adele Ramsey. It's nice to meet you."

They shook hands, exchanged small talk for a few minutes, then the doctor asked Chloe a dozen or so questions before pulling on a pair of latex gloves and beginning her examination.

"From my exam and what you've told me," she said later, as she removed the gloves and lowered the stirrups so that Chloe could sit up, "I'd say you are approximately eight weeks along. Since a normal pregnancy—and I don't anticipate yours will be anything *but* normal—takes anywhere from thirty-eight to forty-two weeks from the date of conception, I think we can safely predict a due date somewhere around January 15th."

Chloe smiled as the realization exploded inside, spreading like a starburst of happiness. She wasn't just having a *baby!* By the end of January, she would be a *mother.*

Oh, my God. I'm going to be a mother.

Tears trembled in her eyes, but these weren't the painful tears of Saturday night. These were tears of joy.

Dr. Ramsey's eyes filled with concern. "Are you all right?" She reached behind her for a box of tissues.

Chloe nodded. "I'm fine. Just…just emotional." She took one of the tissues and dabbed at her eyes. "Sorry. I've been a bit weepy lately. Sometimes because I'm sad, other times because I'm happy."

"That's not unusual, you know. Your body is undergoing major hormonal changes." The doctor went on to describe them. "So don't be alarmed if your emotions are all over the map."

Chloe swallowed. "I'll try not to. But, well…there are other things going on, too." Now *why* had she said that? She did *not* want to get into those other things with the doctor.

"Do you want to talk about it?"

Chloe shook her head. "No, not really. It…talking won't do any good."

The doctor eyed her thoughtfully. "I see from your chart that you're unmarried."

"Yes."

"Is the father in the picture at all?"

"No. And he won't be." In a reflexive action, Chloe put her hands protectively over her stomach.

"I see." Dr. Ramsey's gaze briefly lit on Chloe's hands, then moved up to study her again. "It's not easy, raising a child on your own. I know. I did it myself."

"You did?"

"Yes. My husband died very suddenly and unexpectedly. Our son was only three at the time."

"That must have been hard." Chloe remembered when her uncle Phil had died, how hard it had been for her aunt, and Molly was an adult by then.

"It was terrible," Dr. Ramsey said. "I was still in medical school. I wouldn't have been able to finish or become a doctor without help. Thank God for my mother. She was wonderful. What about your family? Are they supportive?"

"They are, but…" Chloe hesitated.

"But what?"

"Um, the thing is…" Chloe took a deep breath. "I won't be staying in Riverton. In fact, I'm planning to relocate this month."

"Oh, I'm sorry to hear that."

"Me, too. I—I would have liked to be able to continue with you until I have the baby."

"Where are you going…if I may ask?"

So Chloe told the doctor her plans.

"Well, I'm sorry I won't get to see you through your pregnancy. But I can give you a couple of recommendations for excellent ob-gyns that I think you would feel comfortable with."

"Women? I do prefer women doctors."

Dr. Ramsey smiled. "Yes. Women."

Chloe left the doctor's office twenty minutes later, armed with a bottle of prenatal vitamins, a booklet of instructions to follow to ensure a healthy pregnancy and a list of three possible physicians to contact in the Syracuse area.

She was still going over everything she and Dr. Ramsey had discussed as she drove through the downtown section of Riverton. Spying her favorite bakery, she impulsively decided to stop and pick up some of their delicious, fresh bagels to have for her breakfast the next few days. Luckily, she spied a parking spot right in front of the shop.

The bell on the front door tinkled, and tantalizing smells of cinnamon and sugar and yeasty bread assailed her as she entered the shop. There was only one other customer there, and she stood with her back to Chloe in front of the large display case.

Chloe stopped dead. *Oh, good heavens!* The customer was Meredith. Chloe's heart knocked against her chest. She didn't know what to do. She guessed she should have realized Todd and Meredith were probably back by now, but she hadn't, so she hadn't prepared herself for an accidental encounter.

Chloe desperately wanted to turn around and walk out, but Trina Douglas, the owner of the shop, who was waiting on Meredith, looked up and smiled, saying, "Hi, Chloe. Be with you in a minute."

Chloe stood frozen, her mind racing, her heart thudding. She couldn't think how to act or what to say. And for a long moment, it seemed as if Meredith, too, wasn't sure what to do, because she didn't turn around. But then she finally did, and their gazes met.

"Hello, Chloe," Meredith said. Her attempt at a smile fell just short of genuine.

Chloe's emotions were in turmoil. Everything she and Meredith had shared in the past—all the girl talk and helpful suggestions about Chloe's upcoming wedding, all the confidences they'd exchanged and all the times Chloe had believed Meredith was her friend—slammed her. She felt so stupid. Worse, she felt exposed and vulnerable.

And yet, even as she was terrified she would fall apart, from somewhere deep her survival skills kicked in, and she summoned the strength and the anger she needed.

"Hello, Meredith." Her voice was steady. "I see you're back. You're looking great. Marriage must agree with you." Meredith *did* look great—tanned and fit—her slender curves shown off to full advantage in designer jeans, a gorgeous soft aqua crocheted sweater and killer heels. Chloe hated her.

Meredith flushed. "Thanks." Her gaze slid away.

Chloe felt a grim satisfaction at Meredith's discomfort. *Score one for the good guys.* She hoped Meredith felt ashamed. What she and Todd had done was lousy. And even though Todd was the worst offender of the two, Meredith had something to answer for, as well.

Walking over to the display case, Chloe studied the assortment of baked goods and ignored Meredith. Chloe had said her piece, and she was done.

And in that moment, she knew no matter how scared

she might be in the future, no matter what life threw at her, she *would* survive. Okay, so she still had a ways to go in this voyage of self-discovery. And maybe she *wasn't* as strong as she'd imagined. But hadn't she suffered a lot worse and survived? Todd and Meredith's betrayal was a minor blip in her life. Minor.

Besides, she thought with secret satisfaction, she'd gained something wonderful from it, something all her own that they would never know about. Resisting the urge to touch her stomach, she looked up and her gaze met Trina's. Trina's eyes sparkled. If eyes could speak, they were clearly saying, you go, girl.

Trina handed Meredith her package. Meredith hesitated a moment, then turned to Chloe and said, "I, um…hope…um, maybe we could get together for coffee or something."

Oh, yeah, just like we're real friends, huh? "Wouldn't that be nice?" Chloe answered smoothly. As Meredith walked toward the door and reached for the handle, Chloe added, "Give Todd my best."

Trina's smile turned to a huge grin once the door closed behind Meredith. "Good for you," she said. "I'm proud of you."

Chloe smiled, even though now that the encounter was over she felt as if she might throw up.

"I've been wanting to tell you," Trina said, "that I think Todd Hopewell is a first-class jerk."

Chloe shrugged.

"And I think Meredith is nuts to have married him."

Touched by Trina's loyalty, Chloe said, "Thanks, Trina."

Later, as Chloe drove home, she felt she'd somehow turned a corner that day. The worst was over. She'd seen Meredith, and she'd come through the encounter in one piece. And she'd faced her demons and knew what she might have to deal with in the future.

From now on, things could only get better.

Simon arrived at the family home ten minutes before seven. His mother was a stickler for time, and woe to the person who showed up late for any appointment. He saw that Todd's canary-yellow Maserati was already parked in the circular driveway. Noah's van was nowhere to be seen, so he probably hadn't gotten there yet.

Simon pulled in behind the Maserati and got out. The June night was mild, with a light breeze. The air was filled with the scent of newly mown grass, and Simon could see the evidence of the gardeners' work in the freshly weeded flower beds and neatly trimmed edges around the drive and the walkway leading to the front entrance.

Girding himself for the coming encounter with his wayward brother, Simon breathed deeply, told himself no matter what happened he would not lose his temper or say anything he would later regret and climbed the three shallow steps to the front entrance. He rang the doorbell.

A few moments later, the door was opened by Harold, the family's long-time man-of-all-services. Gray-haired, blue-eyed and in his seventies, Harold had, along with Martha, the housekeeper, been the mainstay of the Hopewell family for decades.

"'Evening, Harold," Simon said.

"Good evening, sir." Harold smiled. "The family is in the music room."

Just as the solarium was the place for morning coffee and afternoon tea, the music room was sacrosanct for cocktails. Simon chuckled to himself. He wondered if his mother realized how rigid she was when it came to her rituals.

The low murmur of voices greeted him as he approached the west-facing room that glowed in the last remnants of the setting sun. His mother sat in her favorite place, a pale blue velvet Queen Anne chair, one of a pair that sat at an angle to the Steinway grand piano. She looked elegant in a white crepe dress beaded with crystals and pearls along the V-neckline. As always, Max lay by his mistress's feet. The dog's ears perked up at Simon's entrance. To Larissa's right, Todd and Meredith sat together on a cranberry brocade love seat.

"Hello, Mother...Todd...Meredith." Simon kept his voice as pleasant as possible, even though seeing his brother and his new wife holding hands and smiling as if everything was perfectly normal made him furious for Chloe all over again.

Todd rose, and the brothers shook hands. Simon restrained the impulse to squeeze tighter than was polite. "Welcome home," he said.

Todd grinned. "Thanks."

Meredith stood, too, and Simon kissed her on the cheek. She looked very pretty in a one-shouldered green cocktail dress, but she seemed uncomfortable as they greeted each other. Embarrassed, Simon figured. "Welcome to the family," he said.

"Thank you."

Her eyes met his briefly, and he knew he had guessed right. She *was* embarrassed. Her discomfort made him think more of her, even though he'd always liked her. Still, what she'd been party to—what had been done to Chloe—hadn't been nice.

"I see everyone already has a drink," he said, noting his mother's martini, Todd's whiskey and Meredith's white wine. Walking over to the bar on the far wall, Simon fixed himself a vodka and tonic, added a twist of lime, then rejoined the others.

For several long seconds, an awkward silence settled among them. Then Larissa and Meredith both spoke at once.

"We'll wait until Noah gets here before deciding on a firm date, but I wanted—" Larissa began.

"Have you ever been to Fiji, Simon?" Meredith asked. "Oh, sorry." She turned to Larissa. "I didn't realize you were saying something, Mrs. Hopewell."

"It's fine, my dear. I was just saying that we'll need to decide on a firm date for your reception, but we'd better wait until Noah comes so we can be certain we're all on the same page. I do want everyone in the family to be there."

"What reception?" Simon said, looking at his mother.

"One to celebrate Todd and Meredith's marriage, of course." Her answer was smooth, her eyes cool.

Christ. Simon swallowed a large mouthful of his drink before speaking. "I see." No wonder she'd asked him not to bring up Chloe's name tonight. She'd known he wouldn't be happy about this reception idea. "Don't you think having a public reception is the height of insensitivity, Mother?"

Larissa set her now-empty glass down on the mahogany piecrust table next to her. Her expression was icy. "What in the world are you talking about, Simon?"

Simon met her gaze squarely. "With apologies to Meredith, I think Todd and our family have humiliated Chloe enough already. Is it really necessary to rub her nose in it by throwing a huge party?"

"That is ridiculous," his mother said.

"Come on, Simon. It's not like I left her at the altar," Todd said.

"You might as well have." Simon glanced at Meredith. He did feel bad talking about this in front of her, but it couldn't be helped.

"I'm really sorry if she's hurt," Meredith said. "I...we...didn't mean to hurt her. It...it just seemed to happen."

That was a lame excuse if he'd ever heard one, Simon thought.

Todd put his arm around her. "I love Meredith. You wouldn't have wanted me to marry someone I didn't love, would you?"

Simon could have said that Todd had declared his love for Chloe, too. He could have said that Todd had a tendency to get all excited over one thing, then move on to something newer and *more* exciting. He could have said betraying someone you've professed to love didn't just *happen*. Instead, he gave Todd a look, then drained his glass and moved to the bar to replenish his drink.

"Anyway," Todd said, "I don't know why you're so concerned. Chloe seems fine with what's happened."

Simon swung around. "And you know this how?"

"Meredith saw Chloe today, that's how."

Simon looked at Meredith. "You *saw* her today?"

"Yes, I, um, was at Trina's Bakery and Chloe came in. We, um, talked for a few minutes, and she said to give Todd her best. Honestly, Simon, she really *did* seem fine. Actually, *I'm* the one who was uncomfortable."

If Chloe seemed fine, it's because she's a class act, Simon wanted to say. Damn, he hoped she really was okay. He couldn't imagine that she hadn't been rattled by seeing Meredith. She wouldn't have been human otherwise.

"So you see, Simon," his mother interjected, "there's absolutely no reason not to have a big party to celebrate this wonderful marriage. Now, when would…" But she broke off because at that moment, Noah, accompanied by a tall, slender woman with chin-length brown hair, walked into the room.

Simon always smiled when he saw Noah. Two years younger than Simon and three years older than Todd, Noah had always marched to the tune of a different drummer. He even looked different than his brothers. His hair was a brownish-blond, like Larissa's natural color would be if she didn't lighten it, and his eyes were dark, as some earlier ancestor's must have been. Noah was also a talented musician; he was artistic and creative. Neither Todd nor Simon had inherited any of those traits.

Except for Larissa—subjects always came to the queen, she never went to them—everyone got up and greetings and introductions were exchanged.

"I'd like all of you to meet Anna," Noah said. He pronounced it *Ahh-na.* "Anna Beringer." He draped his arm around her shoulders and beamed.

Simon tried not to be obvious as he studied the newcomer. She was an attractive woman—not pretty, but rather striking with her classically chiseled face and solemn topaz eyes. She wore very little makeup and a simple wine-colored dress that ended just above her knees. On her feet were plain brown heels. "It's a pleasure to meet you," he said.

"Thank you. I've been looking forward to meeting Noah's family." Her eyes were friendly, yet appraising, and she spoke with a slight accent.

German, Simon thought. Either German or Dutch or maybe even French. Not American. At least not by birth.

Drinks were fetched for the newcomers by Harold, who had followed them into the room, while Noah led Anna over to meet Larissa. Simon stood back and watched the play of emotions across his mother's face as she tried to determine just who this woman was and why Noah had brought her to a family dinner party when he'd never done anything even remotely similar before.

Simon figured Noah had finally fallen in love. Certainly he seemed protective of Anna, keeping his hand at her waist as they talked with Larissa, although Anna didn't strike Simon as the type that would need protection. In fact, something about her gave Simon the idea she might be older than Noah, and she was certainly more cosmopolitan, because for all Noah's advantages of birth, in many ways he had remained unspoiled.

"So how did you and Noah meet?" Simon asked Anna when he had the chance.

"We met at the shelter." She sipped at her wine, her gaze meeting Simon's over the rim of her glass.

"Do you volunteer there?"

"I do some pro bono legal work for them."

"Ah, so you're a lawyer."

"Yes." She gave him a slight smile, almost as if she were amused.

Ah, what the hell, he thought. So I'm giving her the third degree. She's obviously not intimidated. "Do you work for a local law firm?"

"Yes. I'm with Dixon and Dixon."

Simon nodded.

"Do you know them?" she asked.

"I do. They're fine lawyers, I hear." Janine Dixon and her younger sister Jennifer specialized in women's cases.

"Two of the finest." Anna took another sip of her wine, and her gaze settled on Noah, who was talking to Todd. Her expression softened as she watched him.

Simon decided he liked Anna. She seemed intelligent and thoughtful, and she wasn't made uncomfortable by silence, yet he sensed that under her quiet surface, there was passion. There would have to be to work for the Dixon sisters. Anna was just the kind of woman Noah *would* be attracted to, Simon felt. He could hardly wait to talk to Noah about her, for she intrigued him.

He wondered what his mother thought about her, for after her first surprised expression when Anna had been introduced, Larissa's face had once more assumed its noncommittal mask. He had a feeling, though, that Anna was not the sort of person Larissa would have picked for Noah. For any of them, for that matter. Anna was entirely too self-possessed. She would not be easy to manipulate. Nor would she be likely to be impressed by Larissa's position, money or influence. Simon suppressed a smile. The evening was getting more interesting by the minute.

Eventually, they all moved into the dining room where Martha was waiting to serve dinner. Larissa sat at the head of the table and motioned for Simon to sit across from her at the foot. To her right were Todd and Meredith. To her left were Noah and Anna.

Simon enjoyed the dinner. Anna and Noah's presence had diffused the earlier tension, and he even discovered he could listen to the discussion centering around the upcoming reception without too much rancor. The food, as always, was excellent, as was the wine.

During the entrée—a perfect paella—Noah even managed to visibly warm their mother by saying, "Hey, Mom, I've been wanting to thank you for the donation you made last month. I can't tell you how much we needed it."

"It was nothing, Noah."

"What do you mean?" he said. "It was terrific. We couldn't have managed without it."

Simon could tell by his mother's expression that she didn't want Noah to make a fuss. Yet after his comment she was definitely more relaxed. In fact, by the time dessert was served, Simon had begun to think the evening hadn't been so bad after all. And if Chloe had been there, with *him* of course, it would have been perfect.

But then, without warning, everything changed.

Harold had just poured each of them a flute of champagne, and Todd stood to make a toast. Smiling down at Meredith, he said, "To my beautiful bride—and the newest member of the Hopewell family."

They all raised their glasses and drank.

Larissa beamed. "I'm so happy that you're part of the family now, Meredith, and I'd like it if you'd call me Larissa."

"Thank you," Meredith murmured.

Larissa began to say something else, but before she could Noah stood. Raising his glass, he said, "I'd like to make a toast, too."

Simon happened to still be looking at his mother and saw her quick frown.

Noah looked down at Anna. "I would like to toast *my* bride, who is actually a *newer* member of the Hopewell family."

Amid the chorus of shocked exclamations, he laughed and added, "Of course, Anna's adamant about keeping her own name, so she'll remain a Beringer, but that's fine with me. In fact, anything she does is fine with me."

With that, he bent down and placed a lingering kiss on his wife's upturned lips.

Chapter Nine

"Guess who I ran into today."

"Who?" Chloe asked. It was Thursday afternoon, and Molly had just called.

"Todd," Molly said.

Chloe had been dreading the thought that *she* might run into Todd somewhere before she left Riverton. "Really? Where were you?"

"At the bank. I left the school early because I'd finished all my reports, and on the way home I stopped to make a deposit. Anyway, I went inside instead of using the drive-through because I needed a new check register. I saw him the minute I walked in. He was standing talking to Jeff Morelli."

"Did he see you?"

"Oh, yeah, he saw me. I had to walk right past him."

"What happened? Did he say anything?"

"He looked around and started to say something, but I cut him dead. I looked right through him and kept on going. Just as if he didn't exist." Molly's voice rang with satisfaction. "As far as I'm concerned, he *doesn't* exist."

Chloe couldn't help smiling. Molly was so loyal.

"Anyway," Molly continued, "by the time I was finished at the counter, he was gone. And good riddance."

This time Chloe laughed.

"I mean it. He's a jerk. I told you that."

"Several times," Chloe said drily.

"I still get so mad when I think about what he did. And the *way* he did it. That was just so…cowardly. Boy, I hope he gets his one of these days. Oh! And guess who *else* I saw?"

"I have no idea. Who?"

"Lucas McKee."

"Is he back?" Lucas and Molly had dated for a while, but then his company had sent him to Iraq and they'd lost touch.

"Yes. He said he'd changed jobs, and how he was back here to stay."

"So how do you feel about that?"

"Well, he asked if he could call me…."

Chloe smiled. She'd always liked Lucas, and she knew Molly had, too. "And?"

"I said I'd like that."

Chloe was glad *somebody's* love life might work out.

"So what were you doing when I called?" Molly said. "Still working?"

It was only four o'clock, and Chloe usually worked until five, sometimes later. "No, I quit early today, too. I've been sorting through some of my stuff."

"What stuff? I told you I'd help you."

"I know, but I was tired of sitting. It felt good to move around a little and do something different. I mainly just went through my books and CDs. Don't worry. There'll be plenty left to do before I move."

"Just as long as you don't try to do everything yourself."

"I'm just doing a little at a time. Quit worrying about me."

"I can't help it. You're *pregnant,* you know."

"As if I could forget."

"Are we still on for the weekend?"

"You're still planning on it, aren't you?" Molly was accompanying Chloe to Syracuse this weekend. While there, Chloe hoped to find a small house to rent. She'd already done some preliminary research on the Internet and had contacted a real-estate agent who would show them around.

"I'm looking forward to it," Molly said. "Even though I wish you'd change your mind, it'll be fun to get away, and I'm glad I'll get to help you pick out a place to live."

"Me, too. I would have hated going alone."

"Oh, before I go, Mom just asked if you'd like to come over tonight and have dinner with us. She's doing a chicken stir-fry."

Earlier Chloe had been thinking she might have to order takeout, because she didn't feel like cooking. "Tell Aunt Jane she's a lifesaver. I'd love to come."

"Good. She said we'll eat at about seven. But come whenever."

"I'll be there by six."

Chloe decided she would feel better if she had a shower before going to her aunt's. Cell phone in hand, she was heading for the stairs when the phone rang again. Checking the display, she saw that this time it was Simon calling. Despite the fact she'd decided she would avoid him from now on, her traitorous heart gave a little skip of pleasure. But she made sure her voice didn't betray it when she answered. "Hello, Simon."

"Hi, Chloe. How are you?"

"I'm fine, thanks."

"I hope you don't mind that I called your business phone, but I tried your home phone and got a recording saying it was disconnected."

"Yes, I decided I don't really need a landline anymore." What did he want? She hoped he wasn't going to invite her to dinner again. Well, at least she had a legitimate reason why she couldn't do anything this weekend.

"Look, I know this is last minute, but I've spent the past hour craving a steak from the Riverton Lodge, and I wondered if I could persuade you to have dinner there with me tonight?"

Chloe was glad she'd just accepted her aunt's invitation because she would have been seriously tempted to say yes to Simon otherwise. "I'm sorry, Simon, I can't. I have other plans."

"Just my luck."

"But thank you for asking me."

"What about this weekend? I have a couple of

tickets for the new play at the Village Playhouse. Would you like to go? We could have an early dinner first, then see the play."

"I'm sorry. I'm not going to be here this weekend." Chloe knew it wasn't necessary to explain herself, but she couldn't seem to stop herself. "Molly's going with me to Syracuse…to house hunt."

"Looks like I'm batting zero, doesn't it?"

"I really *am* sorry." And she was. But even if she hadn't had plans, she would have had to pretend she did. More and more, each time she talked to Simon, she realized just how dangerous her attraction to him was. She couldn't let herself forget that.

Maybe she should have a sign printed up that she could carry with her, something that said Danger Ahead. Better yet, maybe Simon should wear a sign that said Tall, Dark and Dangerous. Chloe was amused by her fantasy, even as she knew there was nothing at all amusing about her situation.

After a wonderful dinner where Chloe ate more than she should have, she was repeating the story of her meeting with Meredith for her aunt's benefit, with constant interruptions and editing from Molly, when Jane said, "And how about Simon? Have you seen him lately?"

Chloe shook her head. "Not since Saturday. He called today, though."

"Oh?" Molly said. "You didn't tell me *that*."

"That's because he called right after you and I hung up."

"What did he want?"

Although Molly had asked the question, Chloe's

aunt Jane looked just as interested in the answer. "He wanted to know if I'd like to go with him to the Riverton Lodge tonight."

"Oh, really?" Jane said.

"Don't look like that, Aunt Jane. He was just hungry for steak and wanted company."

"Yeah, right," Molly said.

"A man like Simon Hopewell could find any number of willing companions," Jane said. "I doubt he just wanted company."

Chloe decided she would not share the rest of her conversation with Simon, because if she told them about the second invitation for the weekend, she would just be giving them more ammunition.

"This isn't good," Molly said. "He's the kind who doesn't give up." She looked at her mother. "What do you think, Mom?"

Chloe's aunt chewed on her lower lip. "I think Simon Hopewell is seriously interested in you, Chloe." Her eyes were worried. "And as Molly said, he's persistent."

Chloe didn't know what to say. For weeks, she'd been telling herself the reason he was paying so much attention to her was because he felt some kind of weird responsibility for her. And maybe that *had* been part of it in the beginning. But things seemed different now. And if she were being really honest with herself, she would have to admit he was acting like a man who *was* interested in her.

What was she going to do if he kept calling her and asking her out? She only hoped she could stay strong.

Because Molly was right. Simon Hopewell never did give up, and it was becoming harder and harder for her to say no to him.

* * *

Simon admired so many things about Chloe: her sense of humor, the way she didn't seem to take herself too seriously, her pride and courage, her strength and independence. And even though she tried to hide it, he also sensed a vulnerability about her. She wasn't quite as tough as she made out, and this glimpse at her softer side made him like her even more.

He stood at his office window and looked out over the surrounding countryside. The rolling hills, the wild flowers and trees, the glimpse of the river snaking along the horizon, the blue sky and puffy clouds—it was a tranquil scene that normally soothed him, especially when he had a knotty problem to solve. But today, because he was thinking about Chloe and how nothing in their relationship was going the way he wanted it to, the scene's magic wasn't working.

He was so deeply engrossed that when Maggie knocked on the frame of the open door between their offices, he actually jumped.

"Sorry. Didn't mean to startle you." She walked in and placed the *Riverton Record* on his desk. She gave him an odd little smile.

He frowned. "What?"

"Check out page two" was all she said before disappearing into her own office.

Curious, Simon sat down at his desk and opened the paper.

And there, right at the top of the second page, was a large photo of Todd and Meredith under a huge headline: Reception to Honor Newlyweds Todd and Meredith

Hopewell. This was followed by a story giving all the details of not only the coming extravaganza but of their "whirlwind courtship," wedding and honeymoon.

Simon swore.

Wasn't it bad enough his mother was having this ill-advised party? Did she have to advertise the whole sorry story? This big splash in the paper was the equivalent of rubbing Chloe's nose in it.

He almost picked up the phone to tell his mother exactly what he thought, but at the last minute decided it wouldn't do any good anyway. The damage was done. The damned announcement was already in the paper for all of Riverton to see. Besides, when and if he talked to his mother about this announcement he wanted to do it in person.

This announcement had settled one thing for him, though. He was not going to attend the reception. He didn't care what his mother said or how upset she might get. He wanted no part of it. Instead, on that night, he would take Chloe out somewhere fantastic.

Except…she didn't *want* to go out with him. She'd made that clear when he called her yesterday. She certainly hadn't suggested a rain check. In fact, after she said she was going to Syracuse for the weekend she'd ended the call pretty fast.

Dammit! In frustration, Simon pounded his fist on his desk so hard papers flew in all directions.

Two seconds later, Maggie, eyes wide, appeared in the doorway. "Are you okay?"

Telling himself getting upset wasn't going to solve anything, Simon turned off his computer and began to gather up the scattered paperwork. "I'm fine. I'm just a bit upset right now. I think I'll take the rest of the day off."

"That's a good idea."

Simon knew Maggie thought he was upset with his mother. Fine. Let her think that. Anyway, he *was* upset with his mother. But he was more upset with himself.

Always before, when he had a problem, he could figure out a way to at least buy himself some time to figure out how to solve it. But that strategy wouldn't work now because time was running out.

Riverton's homeless shelter was fairly quiet by the time Simon walked in. He knew from past visits and from talking to Noah that once breakfast was over all the current tenants who didn't have some kind of paid work were required to attend life skills and job training classes. Once they'd "graduated" from these mandatory courses, they were assigned to various city services as volunteer help.

"Hello, Mr. Hopewell." This cheery greeting came from Caroline Waring, who was a jill-of-all-trades at the shelter.

"Hi, Caroline. Is Noah around?"

She inclined her head toward an open doorway. "He's in his office. Go on back."

"Thanks."

Simon passed the lounge, the library and the director's office. The next office was Noah's. The door was open, and Noah sat at his desk. As usual, the office looked like organized chaos with files and books stacked everywhere.

"Hey, Simon." Noah grinned, looking up from his computer monitor. "What brings you here?"

"I wanted to discuss something with you, and I didn't feel like talking on the phone."

"Well, sit down." Noah indicated a plain wooden chair to the side of his desk. "Want some coffee?"

"No, thanks."

"So what's up?"

"Did you see the announcement in today's paper about Todd and Meredith and the reception Mom is having to celebrate Todd and Meredith's marriage?" Simon said once he was settled.

Noah shook his head. "No. What paper?"

Simon would have grinned if he hadn't been so angry. Noah lived in his own world. "The *Riverton Record.*"

"I guess it's around here somewhere." But Noah obviously didn't care.

So Simon told Noah about the article.

Noah shrugged. "You knew about the reception. We talked about it at dinner Monday."

"Yeah, I know, but that was before she knew *you* were married."

"So…?"

"So doesn't this big splash about their wedding and the party she's having for Todd and Meredith tick you off?"

"Not really. I mean, I don't care about that kind of stuff."

"Hell, Noah, *you* just got married, too. Why weren't you and Anna included in the story? Why isn't your marriage being celebrated at this party?"

Noah shrugged again. "Frankly, I'm glad we're not. I hate that kind of thing, and so does Anna. Why do you think we got married so quietly?"

"That's not the point. Ignoring you and Anna is not right."

"If I'm not upset, why are you? Seriously, Simon, I don't care. This kind of thing is meaningless to me."

"Okay, the truth is ignoring your marriage is only part of what's bugging me. The other part is I think it's rotten the way our family continues to treat Chloe Patterson."

Noah blew out a breath. "Yeah, well, that's Mom for you. She never approved of Chloe."

And she obviously doesn't approve of Anna, either. "I'm going to have it out with her. In fact, when I leave here, I'm going over to the house. But before I did, I wanted to know how you felt about the whole thing."

"I'm sorry, Simon. It just doesn't matter to me."

"And you don't think it'll bother Anna?"

"No, I don't. As a matter of fact, we may not even be here for the reception."

Simon raised his eyebrows. "I thought you told her the date was fine with you."

"I did, but Anna's parents are going to be in Paris at the end of the month, and they've asked us to meet them there. We were thinking this could be our belated honeymoon."

Simon couldn't imagine how his mother would feel about Noah not being there. For a woman who cared so much about appearances, it might not sit well. On the other hand, she might be relieved because she could keep on pretending their marriage didn't exist. "That sounds great. I'd pick a week in Paris over this stupid reception myself."

"Actually, we'll probably be gone at least two weeks. I'm due more than a month of vacation—I haven't taken any in two years—and Anna's caseload is light right now, so it won't be a problem for her, either. We thought after Paris that we'd go to Italy and then maybe on to Greece." Noah grinned. "Some days I think I wouldn't mind staying away forever."

Simon grimaced. "I know the feeling."

"So aside from being ticked off at Mom, how's everything else going?" Noah asked.

Simon shrugged. "Same as always. Working too much."

"You know, I'm sorry I can't help out, but the company—"

"Don't apologize," Simon said, interrupting. "I know the company's not your cup of tea. It's okay. No one forced me to go to work for Dad."

"I know, but it doesn't seem fair that you do so much and I get a big chunk of money every year that I don't earn."

"We *all* get a chunk of money we don't earn. Don't forget that I get a generous salary, too."

"Well, Anna and I talked about it, and I'd be happy to take less of a percentage. I know the company is having some financial issues right now."

"Noah, that's not necessary. You're as much a part of the family as any of the rest of us. After all, Mom doesn't do anything for the company, either."

"That's different."

"It's not different. Besides, I know you give away a lot of the money you get from Hopewell."

Noah threw up his hands. "Okay. I give up. You win." Then he smiled. "On a different subject, you dating anyone now?"

Simon shook his head. "No."

"Ever hear from Alexis?"

"Not lately."

"Isn't there even anyone you're interested in?"

Simon looked at Noah curiously. "Why all the questions? You've never been all that interested in my love life before."

"When I'm happy I want everyone to be happy." His grin turned almost shy. "Anna's great, don't you think?"

"Yes, I do think. I liked her very much."

"She liked you, too. She said you were just as she'd pictured you."

"You were talking about me, huh?"

"Only good things."

Simon had a strong urge to confide in Noah, tell him how he felt about Chloe, see if maybe Noah had some advice for him, but the tendency to keep his private feelings private overrode the need to talk, so he stayed silent on the subject.

A few minutes later, after telling Noah he'd like to take him and Anna to dinner some night soon, he said goodbye, but just as he was walking out the door, Noah called him back.

"Hey," he said, "I just remembered. I'm going to be sitting in with Toby Kerrigan's band Friday night. Why don't you drop by? Anna will be there, and I told Todd and Meredith to come, too."

"Where are you playing?" Simon asked.

"That new club—The Copper Penny—out on Riverton Parkway."

"What time?"

"We'll start about eight."

"I'll try to make it."

After leaving the shelter, Simon headed for his mother's. He wasn't looking forward to the coming confrontation, but sometimes you couldn't ignore things just for the sake of peace.

And that damned announcement in the paper was definitely one of those times.

"What do you want me to do, Simon? Pretend Todd and Meredith *aren't* married?"

"You mean like you're pretending *Noah* isn't married?"

His mother glared at him. "I'm doing no such thing."

"Come on, Mom. This is me you're talking to. And we both know that's exactly what you're doing."

"I didn't know Noah was married when I made my plans for the reception," she said stiffly.

"Maybe not in the very beginning, but you know now. You knew when you called that story in to the paper."

"It was too late to change things then."

"It's never too late to change something like that." He eyed her coldly. "Well, guess what? It doesn't matter. Noah and Anna won't be there, anyway." He waited a heartbeat. "And neither will I."

"What do you mean none of you will be there? Of course you'll be there. This is a family celebration! All of us *have* to be there."

"No, we don't. Noah and Anna will be in Paris. On their honeymoon. He just told me today. And I wouldn't come to that party if you paid me."

"If you're not there, Simon, I will never forgive you."

"That's your choice, Mother." He stood, looked down at her for a long moment during which her furious gaze did not falter, then turned and left the room.

He didn't look back.

Chapter Ten

The trip to Syracuse was so frenetic that Chloe was actually able to forget about that humiliating announcement in the *Riverton Record*. When she'd first seen it, she'd felt as if she'd been slapped. Obviously Todd and Meredith hadn't given her feelings a thought when they'd placed the photo and accompanying "whirlwind romance" story on the first page in the society news section. But did that surprise her after what they'd pulled in California?

After the initial shock wore off a little, she tossed the paper in the trash and told herself she would no longer think about it. If she was now a laughingstock or, even worse, an object of pity in Riverton, so be it. What other people thought about her was out of her control. All she could do was get on with her life and maintain her dignity. After all, *she'd* done nothing wrong.

But it was a blessing she'd scheduled the trip to Syracuse for that weekend, because it gave her something else to concentrate on instead. She and Molly left Riverton early on Saturday morning, ate breakfast on the road and arrived in Syracuse shortly after noon. Chloe phoned Jan Webber, the real-estate agent she'd arranged to meet, to let her know they'd arrived. The woman gave Chloe directions to get to her office. Once there she and Molly studied the printouts Webber had prepared, which showed a list of places for rent within the price range Chloe had given her.

It wasn't until late afternoon that Chloe found the perfect place—half of a duplex near Onondaga Community College in the Westbrook area. The duplex was part of a small complex of about two dozen duplexes and faced an inner courtyard rather than a busy street. Chloe loved that aspect and was also thrilled to see a small fenced yard where she would be able to put a playpen or baby swing.

The rental was in her price range, there were three bedrooms—one of which she could use as her office—and the basement was clean and well lighted. And when she found out there was an on-site twenty-four-hour security service for the complex, she was sold. "I'll take it," she said.

"I'm so relieved," she told Molly that night as they were eating dinner at a highly recommended seafood restaurant.

Molly nodded. "I do feel better about your move now that I've seen where you'll live. It's nice," she admitted.

For some reason, Molly's comment caused Chloe to wonder what Simon would think if he could see the duplex. Would he approve? She knew what Larissa would think. She'd lift her snooty nose in the air and act as if the place was beneath her.

"What's the matter?" Molly asked. "Don't you like your flounder?"

"The flounder's wonderful."

"Then why do you keep frowning?"

"I'm sorry," Chloe said with an embarrassed laugh. "I've been thinking about Larissa Hopewell and how she'd feel if she could see the place where her grandchild is going to be raised."

Molly put her fork down and gave Chloe what she called her "evil eye" but was really just a hard stare. "Will you *stop thinking about those people?* Every time you do, you start to feel bad."

"I know. I'm sorry. It's just that it's hard *not* to think of them." *Especially when Simon keeps calling me.*

"I mean it, Chloe. Stop thinking about them," Molly said. "You're moving on, remember?"

"I know, I know. I will." Chloe turned her attention back to her meal and took a bite of her baked potato.

"I can't help thinking if Simon Hopewell hadn't become part of this equation you wouldn't *have* this problem," Molly said.

Chloe didn't look up. She was afraid if she did that Molly would see the truth in her eyes. "Simon has nothing to do with it." She busily buttered a roll, even though she was beginning to feel full and didn't really want it.

"If you say so." But Molly didn't sound convinced.

Chloe sighed. She raised her eyes and met Molly's dubious gaze. "Seriously, Moll, quit worrying about me. I'm fine."

"I didn't say you weren't *fine*. I said I think Simon Hopewell is the reason you can't seem to put the Hopewells where they belong."

"You're wrong. The reason I keep thinking about them, even when I don't want to, is because I'm carrying a Hopewell baby."

But even as Chloe said this, she knew it wasn't entirely true. And she was afraid Molly knew it, too. The only good thing was she wouldn't be staying in Riverton much longer. And once she'd moved to Syracuse, she would be out of Simon's orbit and finally able to focus on the future and what she had, instead of the past and what she couldn't have.

On Monday afternoon, Simon was driving home from visiting a client in nearby Mohawk when he spied a fruit-and-vegetable stand advertising fresh peaches. Impulsively, he pulled in, thinking he'd buy a basket and give some of them to Maggie.

But the moment he saw the peaches close up, he was reminded of Chloe and the way she'd looked the afternoon they sat out on her back patio. When the afternoon sunlight played across her face, she'd glowed with the same golden, rosy color as the peaches.

He would buy two baskets of peaches and give one of them to her. That would give him the perfect excuse for dropping by. Chloe couldn't possibly take offense. And he would say simply—and truthfully—that the peaches had reminded him of her.

It was after five when he entered the Riverton city limits and turned onto Chloe's street. For the past few days, this area of upstate New York had been experiencing a heat wave, and Simon wished he wasn't still dressed in his business clothes. But he'd felt his gesture with the peaches would seem less spontaneous if he went home first and changed.

Chloe opened the door just as he was thinking about ringing the bell a second time. "Hello, Simon." Her eyes seemed guarded as she greeted him. And yet, wasn't that a spark of pleasure he'd glimpsed in their depths just before the shutter came down?

"I hope I'm not interrupting. I come bearing gifts," he said lightly. God, she looked gorgeous to him with those wavy tendrils of hair escaping her ponytail and her skin so fresh and creamy and healthy looking. She didn't even need makeup, although she still had traces of light red color on her lips—color he imagined she'd applied that morning. Did she have any idea how sexy she was? He couldn't understand why there weren't droves of men lined up on her doorstep.

Her gaze moved to the loaded basket he held out. "You brought me peaches?" she said. "Why?"

"I saw these at a produce stand. They reminded me of you."

Faint color stained her cheeks as their eyes met again. This time she didn't attempt to disguise her pleasure. "Thank you." She only hesitated a few seconds before adding, "Would you like to come in for a minute?"

"I *would* like to hear about your trip to Syracuse. But are you sure I won't be keeping you from something?"

She shook her head. "No, I had just finished up for the day and was going to get a glass of iced tea."

By now he was inside, and she had taken the basket of peaches.

"C'mon into the kitchen," she said.

A few minutes later, he'd shed his jacket and tie and, armed with a cold beer, he followed her out back where they once again sat on her patio. Today the breeze was very warm—the temperature had climbed into the high eighties that afternoon—but the shaded area felt comfortable.

"So tell me all about the house-hunting trip," he said after taking a long swallow of the beer.

As she talked, he watched the play of emotions across her expressive face and thought anew how much he wished things were different between them. He knew the odds were against him where Chloe was concerned, yet he wasn't willing to give up. No, that wasn't quite right. He *couldn't* give up.

The simple truth was, he was falling in love with Chloe. This wasn't a game he was playing where the only goal was winning. This was his life and his future.

No matter what his family thought, no matter what they said, no matter how any of them might object, he wanted to see if there was any possibility of a future with her.

He was thinking so hard he hadn't noticed she'd stopped talking. "Sorry," he said, "I guess my mind wandered. So you rented a townhouse, you said?"

"Half of a duplex," she corrected.

"And where, exactly, is it?"

"Out in the suburbs. It's a nice area. Molly liked it."

He wondered if she thought he hadn't noticed how evasive her answer was. She obviously didn't want him to know where she was going to be living. Didn't she know how easy it was to find someone nowadays? Especially when that someone had a business advertised over the Internet and through her clients' Web sites?

"Good," he said. "I'm glad you found something you liked." He waited for her to comment, and when she didn't, he said, "I've been wanting to tell you that my brother Noah has gotten married."

"Really?"

"Yes. Big surprise to everyone."

"Who'd he marry? Anyone I know?"

"I doubt it. Her name is Anna Beringer, and she's a lawyer in Janine and Jennifer Dixon's firm."

"Is she from around here?"

"No. She moved to Riverton a couple of years ago. She's originally from Germany, but she came to the United States with her parents when she was in her teens."

"How'd they meet?"

"She's a lawyer and does pro bono work at the shelter. They've been dating for about six months, and last week they just up and eloped."

"What did your mother think of that?"

Simon grinned. "Let's just say this development has shaken her up."

"I'll bet," she said drily. She turned to look at him. "And has an announcement been in the paper yet?"

"No." He waited a heartbeat. "I suppose you saw the

one about Todd and Meredith and the party my mother is throwing."

"Who hasn't?" she said, her voice cool now.

He knew she was hurt, but what could he say? Still, he had to try. "Look, Chloe," he began, "I know—"

"You know, Simon, I don't want to talk about that story. And I really need to get busy." She stood. "I've begun my packing, and it's going to take a lot longer than I thought." She smiled, but the smile didn't reach her eyes. "Thank you so much for the peaches."

Damn. "I hope you enjoy them." He rose to leave. He'd have liked to stay longer, but he knew Chloe was wary of him—with good reason—and he didn't want to cause her to become even more cautious. What he wanted was for her to trust him. To realize he would never hurt her. And to acknowledge what was growing between them, whether she had faced it yet or not. If that took time, well, he would be patient, even if it took years, even if it meant he would spend every moment of his free time for the foreseeable future in Syracuse.

Chloe was worth it.

Because Molly insisted, Chloe agreed that on Friday night she would accompany her cousin and a couple of her teacher friends to a new club that had opened a couple of miles north of Riverton.

"It's supposed to be a great place. They've got a live band and everything," Molly said.

"But, Moll, I can't drink now, and I hate loud music."

"Oh, come on. It'll do you good to get out. Anyway,

everyone's been raving about their food. Their burgers, especially, are supposed to be fantastic."

"Just what I need. Fantastic burgers," Chloe said drily. She'd already gained five pounds, and she was only two months along. She hated to think where she'd be by the end of her pregnancy.

"And don't say you don't have anything to wear," Molly said, anticipating Chloe's next excuse. "Wear your red sundress. It looks great on you."

Chloe grumbled, but she gave in.

Deciding Molly was right about the red sundress— it would be more comfortable than pants, most of which were feeling a bit snug—Chloe paired the dress with flat red sandals and took along a white crocheted shawl to throw over her shoulders in case the club's air-condtioning was on full blast.

Molly said Terri, one of her teacher friends, had offered to drive and pick them all up. They agreed they would go early so they could have dinner before the band began to play. When Terri came by for Chloe, Molly and the other teacher, who introduced herself as Hannah, were already in the SUV. When they walked into The Copper Penny—named for the owner's wife Penny, they found out later—Chloe saw that the place was already at least half-full, so obviously others had had the same idea about getting there early. All the tables nearest the dance floor were already taken, which suited Chloe just fine. The four of them ended up at a table on the far side of the room. Too many people were in front of them to have a clear view of the small stage where the band was setting up, but Chloe didn't mind.

She glanced around. She saw a few people she recognized but no one she knew well, which was actually a relief. She wasn't in the mood to fend off questions about Todd and Meredith or anything else, especially that awful story in the *Record*. In fact, now that Molly had talked her into coming tonight, she figured she might as well enjoy herself as much as possible. To that end, when they placed their order for drinks and food, she decided to splurge and have some of the club's highly touted skinny fries along with her burger and soft drink. If she was going to get fat, anyway, why not enjoy it?

The place quickly filled up until every table seemed to be occupied. "Nice crowd, isn't it?" Chloe said.

"It's a great crowd," Molly said, looking around. "Looks like this place is going to be a success."

"We needed a place like this after Rocky's closed," Terri said. She was a lively blonde who wore her hair in one long braid. When Chloe asked, she said she was a chemistry teacher and, like Molly, she was also teaching summer school.

They had just been served their food when the band arrived. By the time they'd set up and finished their sound check, Chloe had eaten as much as she wanted and pushed the rest away.

As soon as the band swung into their first piece, Chloe realized they were good. She enjoyed listening to them, even though she couldn't see them very well. They played music similar to Coldplay, kind of a cross between U2 and the Beatles, she thought.

Before long Terri and Hannah were asked to dance, and they joined the other couples on the dance floor. As soon as they left the table, Molly leaned over and said, "Chloe, isn't that Noah Hopewell playing one of the guitars?"

Chloe strained to see around the table blocking her view. Oh, Lord, it *was* Noah. How could she not have seen him when the band came in? For a moment, she felt panic, but it quickly disappeared. So what if he was here playing? She'd only ever met Noah once, and that was last year at a big Christmas party. He probably didn't even remember her. And even if he did it was no big deal. In fact, if he saw her enjoying herself, he might say something to Todd or Meredith. Even the thought gave her satisfaction. Of course, with those lights shining in his eyes, he probably couldn't see anything.

"You're not upset, are you?" Molly asked.

"Absolutely not," Chloe said.

A few minutes later, a former high-school classmate of Chloe's walked over to their table and asked her if she'd like to dance. She looked at Molly to see if she'd mind.

"Go," Molly urged.

"Are you sure?" Chloe hated sitting alone at a table when everyone else was dancing.

"I'm sure. Besides," Molly added, grinning, "I'll eat the rest of your French fries while you're gone."

Chloe laughed, and the classmate, whose name was Kevin, led her out onto the floor.

Chloe found she actually *was* enjoying herself once they began to dance. She'd always loved dancing, and she'd had little opportunity to do much of it while she and Todd were together. Dancing was one skill he hadn't possessed, which had surprised her. In fact, he actively disliked it and had refused to even try unless the music was super slow, saying he preferred to watch everyone else. *I should have known then he wasn't right for me.*

"You're a great dancer," Kevin said as they danced to a number with a Latin beat.

"Thanks. You're pretty good yourself."

The song ended, and a slower one began. After glancing in the direction of their table and seeing that Molly was also dancing now, Chloe relaxed and settled into Kevin's arms.

She looked over his shoulder as they slow danced to a romantic ballad when she saw several new people enter the club. It took a moment for it to register in her brain that two of the newcomers were Todd and Meredith.

Her heart gave a thud of alarm. She closed her eyes as if shutting out their images would cause them to disappear. *Oh, God.* What was she going to do? Could she handle this? They were bound to see her. *But they won't come over to talk to me. Will they?* Surely not. Telling herself to be calm, she opened her eyes and strained to see where they were. *Please God, let them be way on the other side of the room somewhere.* Relief flooded her as she saw that they were indeed seated way across the room at a table close to the band but not right on the dance floor. Chloe had noticed the table earlier because only one woman was sitting there. It was obvious Todd and Meredith knew the woman because they were talking and laughing with her.

"Is something wrong?" Kevin asked, pulling back a ways so he could look at her.

Chloe realized she had tensed up since spying Todd and Meredith and willed herself to relax again. "No, of course not," she said.

But the rest of the song was agony for her, and when it was over, she immediately turned to go back to her table. It was one thing to tell herself it didn't matter that Todd and Meredith were there and that she should relax; it was quite another to actually do it.

She thanked Kevin, told him she'd enjoyed dancing with him and sat down. He seemed bewildered by her change of mood but didn't protest. She tried to get her emotions under control as she waited for the rest of the set to be over and for Molly to return.

But Molly and her partner stayed on the dance floor for the next set, too. The only one of their group to join Chloe was Hannah. She sank into her chair and smiled at Chloe.

"Do your feet hurt, too?" she asked.

"No, I'm just tired."

"Yeah, Fridays are like that."

Chloe nodded, but her mind was spinning in all directions. If only she could leave.

Molly finally came back to the table, and Chloe leaned over to say in her ear, "Todd and Meredith are here."

Molly's eyes widened, and she stared at Chloe. "Are you okay?"

Chloe nodded.

"Are you sure? Because I could ask Terri to take you home. She wouldn't mind."

Chloe shook her head. Running into Todd and Meredith had to happen sometime. She could stick it out. It wasn't as if she had to talk to them or anything.

Molly stayed by her side during the next set, but when Lucas McKee stopped by their table and asked her to dance, Chloe encouraged Molly to go. She knew Molly still had a bit of a crush on Lucas.

Chloe surreptitiously watched the table where Todd and Meredith were sitting, even though in the crush of the crowd and the distance between her table and theirs, they probably hadn't even seen her. At one point, Meredith got up and seemed as if she were headed Chloe's way, and Chloe tensed, but Meredith headed off in the direction of what Chloe imagined was the ladies' room, and Chloe relaxed again.

When the set was over, the band announced they were taking a fifteen-minute break, and Chloe saw that Noah Hopewell walked right over to the table where Todd and the unknown woman sat. When Noah got there, he pulled out a chair next to the woman and then leaned over and kissed her.

Oh. That must be his wife.

Chloe wished she could see the woman better, but they were too far away and it was too dark in the club. Within minutes, Meredith returned and joined them.

"What's happening over there?" Molly asked. "Who's the woman?"

"I think she must be Noah's wife," Chloe said.

She and Molly watched for a while, and Chloe couldn't help but think how that could have been her at that table. The funny thing was that the thought didn't make her feel bad. She knew she was better off without Todd. If not for the baby she carried, she wouldn't care at all. Now if it had been Simon she'd been engaged to…

Don't go there. You think about Simon entirely too much.

Not two minutes later, almost as if she'd conjured him, she saw Simon enter the club. This time her heart banged against her chest. She wasn't sure if she wanted to sink down and hide so he wouldn't see her or if she *wanted* him to see her.

And the odd thing was that as he stood there in the entrance looking around, he *did* see her. She knew the moment her presence registered, for his head became motionless and their eyes met across the room. Even from this distance, she could see the smile play across his lips, and her breathing quickened.

He began to weave his way through the tables toward her. When he was about halfway there, the band began to play again. Chloe could feel Molly staring at her. When Simon was within a foot or so of their table, Chloe slowly stood.

"Chloe!" Molly said urgently. "What are you doing?"

Simon just stood there, a question in his eyes.

Without taking her gaze from Simon's, Chloe stepped forward and put her hand in his.

Chapter Eleven

Chloe felt as if she were in some kind of dream as she and Simon moved onto the dance floor. She was thankful the music was slow, because she needed the strength of Simon's arms just then.

She knew that at least two tables full of people were staring at them. There must be raised eyebrows, dropped jaws, incredulous or outraged murmurings. None of it mattered. The crowd receded, and just for a few moments she allowed herself to take what she wanted.

What she needed.

Chloe sighed and rested her head against his chest and swayed to the sweet guitar music. Just this once.

"Are you all right, Chloe?"

"I am now." She raised her eyes, and their gazes locked.

"I hope that means what I think it means."

Her heart was beating so fast. Could he feel it?

"I…" She took a deep breath. "You make me feel safe."

In answer, he held her closer, and now she could feel *his* heart beating. She knew the way she was behaving was crazy, that there couldn't possibly be any kind of future for her with Simon, that she was only making more problems for herself than she already had…yet she felt powerless to stop herself.

She needed this man.

She especially needed him now.

Tonight had shown her, as nothing else could have, that Simon made her feel she could face anything and anyone as long as she was in his arms.

The song ended, but he kept his arms around her.

"Did you drive tonight?" he murmured in her ear.

"No."

"Do you want to get out of here?"

She leaned back so she could see him and nodded.

"Let's go, then."

"I have to get my purse, and I have to tell Molly," she said.

"Do you want me to come with you?"

"No. I-I'll meet you by the door."

He squeezed her hand, then allowed her to walk away.

"Chloe," Molly said when Chloe told her Simon was taking her home, "are you sure you know what you're doing?"

"I'm sure." But all Chloe was really sure of was that no matter what happened tomorrow or all the other tomorrows in her life, as least she would have tonight.

* * *

Simon hadn't wanted to go to the club, but he'd halfway promised Noah, so at eight o'clock, when he remembered Noah's invitation, he decided he would drive out there, and even if he only stayed a little while, at least he would have made an appearance.

He'd seen his brothers first, sitting with their wives. He'd been about to walk to their table, but then he'd spied Chloe. He'd been stunned, and his heart had leaped with happiness.

He'd immediately started toward her, almost as if someone else was guiding him. He'd given no thought to what his brothers would think. All he cared about was Chloe. And the unbelievable thing was that Chloe seemed just as happy to see him and that she had agreed to let him drive her home.

As he drove slowly back to town, he was all too aware of her sitting next to him. He could smell the light fragrance she wore; he could almost feel the warmth of her body. Her skin glowed in the moonlight—skin he ached to touch. He wondered if she had any idea how she made him feel.

He wished he knew what to say. They hadn't talked since they'd gotten into his car.

What was she thinking? Her face was turned away from him. Was she upset? She'd said he made her feel safe. Did she still feel that way? Or was she sorry she'd left with him?

"Simon," she said, startling him.

He swallowed. "You doing okay?"

"Yes, I—I'm fine. I just…wanted to thank you for rescuing me."

"Any time," he said lightly.

She sighed deeply. "I was really rattled by seeing Todd and Meredith tonight. I never would have gone to the club if I'd known they would be there."

"I know." Hell, who *would* want to see the two people who had betrayed you? Only someone as insensitive as they were, and Chloe was anything but. "Noah doesn't play with that band all the time. He was just sitting in tonight. He asked us all to come."

"Just my luck," she said. "Anyway, thank you. I—I owe you one."

Although he wanted to reach over and take her hand and tell her he'd do anything in the world for her, he knew he'd better keep it light. Otherwise, he might scare her off for good. "Then maybe one of these days you'll let me take you to dinner instead of always saying no."

"Maybe."

But he could hear in her voice that she was already regretting the way she'd acted earlier, the way she'd let him see that she had feelings for him. He'd have to think of something fast—some way to ensure he would see her again.

They got to her house much too soon. Simon was still trying to figure out how to press his advantage—an advantage he might never get again—when he pulled up in front and parked.

He was out of the car and around to the passenger side before she had a chance to open the door herself.

He reached for her hand to help her out, and the feel of her smaller palm in his was enough to make him itch to haul her into his arms and kiss her senseless.

He kept hold of her hand as they walked to her front door, and after some initial resistance, she made no effort to pull away. Yet when they stopped, she said softly, "I'm sorry if I gave you the wrong impression. I—I'm not going to ask you in."

He made no effort to mask his disappointment. "Chloe…"

"Please don't make this any harder than it is already."

In the moonlight, he could see tears glistening in her eyes. And then, while he was still trying to think what he could say to change her mind, she raised up on her tiptoes and kissed him.

He knew she meant the kiss to be light—a goodbye. But he couldn't let her go like that. Instead, he crushed her to him and deepened the kiss. Almost immediately, she melted against him, and the warmth of her mouth, the softness of her lips, the feel of her tongue tangling with his, all forced him to exercise a willpower he hadn't known he possessed. Because as much as he wanted to keep her right where she was, as much as he wanted to keep kissing her until he banished every single one of her doubts, as much as he wanted to make his mark so that, despite everything against them, she would know they belonged together—he also knew he couldn't rush her. She'd made the first tentative move toward him, but he knew she would bolt if he tried to force more than she was willing to give.

* * *

Safely inside, with the door shut behind her, Chloe sagged against the wall and trembled. She heard Simon's footsteps as he walked away. Heard the thunk of his car door. Heard the low growl of his ignition.

As the sound of the Lexus faded away, she sank to the ground. The tears she'd held back slipped down her face.

Letting Simon leave had been one of the hardest things Chloe had ever had to do. More than anything, she'd wanted to bring him inside, to close the door against the outside world, to let him make love to her. She wrapped her arms around herself as if she could stave away the sudden flood of loneliness and the need that thrummed through her.

I'm falling in love with him.

Maybe I'm already in love with him.

But how could that be? Less than a month ago she'd been engaged to marry Todd. And now she was in love with his *brother?*

No wonder Molly thinks I'm nuts.

But no matter what anyone thought, Chloe knew it was true. She had fallen in love with Simon Hopewell.

I might as well have fallen in love with some famous movie star, for all the good it will do me. Because any relationship between Simon and Chloe was just as pre-posterous…and just as hopeless.

The next day she awakened early. No matter what had happened, she could not afford to sit around and feel sorry for herself. She had too much to do.

She'd earmarked today for serious packing. Just ten

days from today she was scheduled to move, so there was no time to waste. At the very least, she wanted to get most of her kitchen packed up today.

She had barely fixed her first cup of coffee when her cell phone rang with the distinctive ringtone that meant the caller was Molly. Chloe sighed. She loved her cousin dearly, but she wasn't sure she was ready for the third degree she knew she was going to get.

"Good morning, Molly," she said.

"Did I wake you?" Molly said.

"No. I was just about to drink my first cup of coffee."

"I couldn't wait another minute! What happened? Why did you leave with Simon last night?"

Chloe sighed again. She had a feeling she'd have a headache by the time this conversation was over. "I left because it was too uncomfortable for me to stay."

"But I told you earlier that I'd ask Terri to take you home if you wanted to go, and you said no!"

"Look, I didn't want to make a big deal out of it. Asking Terri to take me home would have attached too much importance to me leaving. I certainly didn't want to have to explain anything to Terri. Nor did I want to lie to her and make up some fake excuse."

"And you thought leaving with Simon Hopewell was a *better* option?"

"Yes, I did."

"Chloe, have you forgotten that you're pregnant with Todd's baby?"

Chloe closed her eyes. "How could I forget?" *Especially when you remind me constantly.* She knew that thought was unfair. She knew Molly only cared about her welfare. Yet Chloe found herself resenting Molly's questions.

"I don't know," Molly said. "But I'm just worried about where you're going with this."

"Well, stop worrying. I'm an adult. I know what I'm doing."

"I'm not sure you do. Even Mom—"

"What? Have you already told Aunt Jane about last night?" Now Chloe wasn't just resentful. She was angry.

"Well, yeah, I—"

"You know, Moll," Chloe interrupted, "sometimes I'd really like to have a bit of privacy."

Silence.

"I…" Chloe took a deep breath. Told herself that Molly meant well. Told herself that the last thing she wanted to do was alienate her cousin or hurt her feelings. "Look, I have a lot to do today. And I'm tired of talking about this. If it makes you feel better, nothing happened last night. Simon drove me home. Period. He didn't come in. Just said good-night and went home. There. Does *that* make you happy?" Chloe ignored the little voice that said she wasn't really telling the whole truth. But it was none of Molly's business—or *anyone's* business—that Simon had kissed her last night.

"I…just hope…oh, never mind. You know how I feel."

"Yes, I do."

"I—I'm sorry, Chloe. I just care about you. I hope you know that."

"I do," Chloe said in a softer voice.

"So," Molly said more heartily, "what time do you want me to come over and help you?"

"I honestly don't need any help today." Chloe wouldn't have minded help, but she absolutely could not stand one more question or comment about Simon Hopewell.

"Are you sure?"

Chloe knew she had hurt Molly's feelings, and she was sorry about that. But she wasn't going to change her mind. "I'm sure."

"Okay. Um, do you still want to go see that new Hugh Jackman movie tomorrow?"

"Maybe. I'll call you."

Chloe stood looking at the phone after they'd hung up. For the first time ever, she wondered if putting some distance between her and Molly might actually be a good thing. Because even when you loved someone— even when you knew they meant well—you could still begin to feel a little bit annoyed by their constant interference in your life.

Deciding she would put Molly and her comments out of her mind, at least for now, Chloe turned her attention to her breakfast and her plans for the day.

By nine o'clock, she was hard at work. When her cell phone rang for the second time that morning, she was startled to see Simon's name on the caller ID. She debated whether to let the call go to voice mail, but she was too curious about what he might have to say so she answered.

"How are you this morning?" he said.

"I'm fine. How are you?"

"Wondering what you have planned for the day."

"I'm packing. The entire day."

"I had a feeling that's what you'd say."

"Yes, I still have a lot to do. And I can't afford to do

any of it during the week because I can't neglect my clients." Chloe knew she was talking too much, saying more than she needed to, but that's what happened when she got nervous.

"I'm coming over to help."

"What? No, Simon, that's not—" she began.

"I'll be there in thirty minutes," he said, interrupting her.

Before she could answer, he broke the connection. Chloe stared at the phone. She wasn't sure if she was angry over his high-handed treatment or if she was grateful he had taken charge of the situation. One thing she did know was those darned butterflies were back.

As always, Simon was right on time. Her doorbell rang precisely thirty minutes later. Chloe, with her hair freshly arranged and her face made up, answered the door.

Just the sight of him in his well-worn jeans and form-fitting gray T-shirt was enough to start her heart beating too fast. When their eyes met, she couldn't help remembering how it had felt to be kissed by him last night, and she knew he was thinking about the same thing, for his gaze immediately went to her lips then slowly came back to meet her gaze again.

"Hi," she said. She knew she was blushing.

"Hi." His smile said everything he didn't say aloud.

Chloe told herself to breathe. "C'mon in." She stood back.

His arm brushed against her as he walked past, and the hairs on her arm rose. She shivered. She was such a mess.

"Okay, put me to work," he said.

She beckoned for him to follow her to the kitchen,

where she already had several large kitchen cartons taped together and ready to be packed. On the kitchen table lay a stack of brown wrapping paper. "You can do that cabinet. That's where all the heavier pots and pans are. And that big box is the heavy-duty one, so that's where they should go. I'm going to work on the glassware and china."

For the next couple of hours they worked companionably side by side. She immediately recognized that Simon knew how to pack and that he'd do a good job, so she didn't have to watch him and could get on with her own work. They wrapped and packed and sealed and labeled, and by one o'clock, they were almost finished with the kitchen.

"I'm hungry," Simon said, putting down the tape he'd been using.

"Are you?" Chloe thought about how bare the refrigerator was. She didn't think he'd care for a Lean Cuisine, which was about all she ever ate for lunch.

"I vote for Chinese food," he said. "I'll go get it. What do you like?"

"Lemon chicken and any kind of lo-mein noodles or dumplings."

He grinned. "I knew you were a gal after my own heart. I'll be back in about half an hour." As he walked out of the kitchen, he said, "Keep the home fires burning."

Chloe laughed. "I'll do my best."

He came back with two big bags that contained not only the lemon chicken she'd asked for, but a lo-mein noodle dish filled with vegetables and shrimp, pan-fried dumplings and beef and broccoli. There was also a big container of hot-and-sour soup, four crispy egg rolls, lots of rice and fortune cookies.

"It's a feast!" Chloe said. She'd mixed up some iced tea while he was gone so they were all set.

It was fun to sit at the kitchen table and stuff themselves with Chinese food. It felt to Chloe like they might be an old married couple. It seemed natural and comfortable and homey. She tried to think if she and Todd had ever done anything like this, but she couldn't remember anything even remotely similar. Todd had always wanted to go out to expensive places. He'd even disdained Rosa's, and Rosa's had the best Italian food in the vicinity.

Reluctantly, she finally rose and began to clean up. Immediately Simon got up and helped. There was enough food left to save and have for lunch tomorrow, and Chloe was grateful she could reuse the original cartons since she and Simon had packed most of her storage containers.

When they were finished with the cleanup, he said, "What else do you want me to do?"

"Would you like to pack up my little tool shed for me?"

"You have a tool shed?"

"Yes, didn't you see it on my patio? Come on. I'll show you."

Ten minutes later he was working away outdoors, and Chloe was going through her pantry and making three piles: one to keep for use until she moved, one to pack up and the other to give to her aunt because it would not pack well.

By four o'clock, Simon was finished outside, and Chloe had filled a good-size trash bag in the kitchen.

"I'm beat," Chloe told him when he came inside. "I think it's time to quit for the day." She smiled. "I can't thank you enough. Now I really owe you."

"I told you. Let me take you to dinner."

"I'm too tired tonight."

"Tomorrow then. We'll go to the Riverton Lodge and get that steak."

Chloe wanted to say yes. Was there really any harm in going out to dinner with him? Soon she would be gone, and the entire Simon problem would disappear. "That actually sounds wonderful," she said.

"Good. I'll pick you up at six."

A few minutes later, they'd said their goodbyes, and Simon left. It was only then that Chloe remembered she'd half promised Molly she'd go with her to see the new Hugh Jackman movie. She made a face. Molly wouldn't care that Chloe was breaking a tentative date because of a chance to go out with an attractive man— Molly would do the same thing herself and it wouldn't bother Chloe in the least—in fact, she'd encourage her cousin to go.

But Molly *would* care that the man was Simon.

And Chloe thought that Molly would be right.

Chloe had wanted to say yes, so she'd rationalized why it would be okay to accept Simon's invitation. But it wasn't okay. And Chloe knew it. By all her actions the past two days, Chloe had sent a message that Simon's attentions were welcome. What she was doing to him was unfair. And it was dishonest.

Because no amount of rationalizing would change the facts. There was no future for her with Simon.

Chapter Twelve

Chloe had to admit it was fun to get dressed up and ready for a date to a fancy restaurant. It had been a while since she'd primped for a night out—more than two months—since well before Todd had left for California.

She'd been to the Riverton Lodge several times with him, but she was a lot more excited about going tonight with Simon. She decided to wear a dress she'd bought last year for a Christmas party but had not worn. The dress was black crepe, almost a straight line from shoulders to just above the knees, with only a slight indentation at the waist. It was sleeveless, and the neckline was squared off and trimmed with a wide satin collar studded with black brilliants. The hemline also sported the same sparkly black satin trim. The dress made her feel elegant and sophisticated, and it had the added benefit of a looser fit, which camouflaged her newly acquired five pounds.

With it she wore high-heeled sandals made of thin black straps also studded with tiny, sparkling black stones. Square black onyx earrings and black bangle bracelets completed her outfit. She would also take along a silvery woven silk shawl in case the restaurant was too cold.

After much thought, Chloe decided to put her hair up. She didn't wear it up often, but tonight seemed to call for the more sophisticated look. To soften the look just a bit, she allowed a few tendrils to escape and trail down her neck.

She kept her makeup simple. Smoky eye shadow, dark mascara, just a hint of blush high on her cheekbones and a shimmery claret lipstick. She sprayed her favorite perfume in the air and walked through it. Then she added a bit more to her pulse points.

Standing in front of the full-length mirror on the back of her bedroom door, she assessed her overall appearance. Not half-bad, she thought with a grin. She hoped Simon would approve.

His eyes told her he *did* approve, very much. He echoed the sentiment by saying, "Wow. You look gorgeous."

Giving him a small curtsy, Chloe said, "Thank you. You don't look so bad yourself."

In fact, she'd give him an A+. Tonight he wore a dark charcoal suit that looked like cashmere to her, paired with a pale gray shirt and a gray-and-white-striped tie. Combined with his almost black hair and gray eyes, he looked as if he could be a model for *GQ*.

Chloe grabbed her black beaded evening bag, and they were off. The drive to the restaurant took about forty minutes. They didn't talk much. Chloe was very aware of Simon next to her, but she willed herself to relax and listen to the Luciano Pavarotti CD Simon had chosen and not worry about anything except enjoying the moment.

When they arrived at the Riverton Lodge, which was surrounded by lighted trees reminiscent of Tavern on the Green in Manhattan, Simon pulled into the curved drive and allowed the valet parking attendant to take over while he came around and helped Chloe out of the car and up the three shallow steps to the main entrance of the restaurant.

Soft music from the string quartet that played at the Lodge on Friday and Saturday nights greeted them as they entered. The hostess, a beautiful redhead dressed in royal blue, greeted them with a warm smile. "Hello, Mr. Hopewell. We're so glad to see you again." Her gaze flicked over Chloe.

"Thanks, Danielle."

"We have your table ready." Her smile was brilliant.

Chloe noticed that the smile didn't include her. In fact, there was something in the hostess's gaze that told Chloe she'd probably recognized her and knew about her aborted engagement to Todd. Small towns were like that. No secrets possible. She decided to ignore the woman.

Their table was tucked into a corner by one of the

huge windows overlooking the back of the restaurant. The same lighted trees illuminated the grounds, which were filled with flowering shrubs and paved walkways. During the daytime, visitors were encouraged to walk around after they'd eaten. Even at night, a few couples could be seen strolling hand in hand. Chloe knew there were fountains dotted here and there and that, if you were lucky, you might hear a nightingale singing. Beyond the copse of trees was a small lake. It was a beautifully kept property. It was no wonder the prices were so high.

Simon held Chloe's chair out for her.

The hostess left them, saying, "Phillip will be by shortly."

"Phillip is the sommelier," Simon explained as he sat across from Chloe.

Chloe nodded.

Simon picked up the wine list.

"I won't be drinking wine tonight," Chloe said, figuring she might as well make that clear right away. "So don't worry about me."

Simon's eyes met hers. "Don't you drink at all?"

"Sometimes I do. Why? Does it bother you that I don't want any wine?"

"No, of course not. I just wondered, that's all."

In other words, it had crossed his mind that maybe she had a drinking problem. But perhaps that was unfair. It *was* unusual for a person to refuse to have a glass of wine with a nice dinner, Chloe imagined. She wished she could explain why she wasn't drinking anything right now. Oh, sure. What would she say? By the way, Simon, there's something I've been meaning to tell you…

He'd be appalled. And he'd be angry. He might even decide to take her home and forget about dinner. But no, that was ridiculous. Simon would never behave that way. He was too kind and too much of a gentleman. Yes, he would be shocked, and he might be angry, but he would also understand exactly why she'd been resisting him so hard. And why there could never be anything permanent between them.

Immediately, some of the joy in the evening evaporated.

"Something wrong?" he asked.

Chloe blinked. She had to stop doing that. She had to stop thinking about her situation, especially when she was in Simon's company. He was too sharp. Too perceptive. What if he guessed?

"No, not at all. I guess I was just daydreaming. It's so beautiful here." She looked around, her gaze sweeping over the plush carpeting, the floor to ceiling windows, the rich appointments everywhere.

"You've been here before, surely?"

"Yes, but…well, it's particularly beautiful tonight."

His smile softened. "From where I sit, the view is gorgeous."

Chloe was glad the lights were so low and that he couldn't see the blush that flared. His meaning was clear. But hadn't she meant the same thing? Her heart skipped. *Careful. Careful.*

When the sommelier returned, Simon ordered his wine, as well as a bottle of sparkling water for her. Soon their waiter, a handsome young man who introduced himself as Ryan, brought them a basket of hot rolls and a dish of butter. "I'll be back soon to take your orders," he said.

"No hurry," Simon said.

Chloe agreed. She didn't want to rush the evening. This would be her only chance to spend such a lovely time with Simon, and she intended to make the most of it.

They chatted about nothing in particular and then placed their orders. Both of them wanted steak, although Simon chose the New York strip and Chloe chose the petite filet.

Chloe buttered a roll to eat while they were waiting for their salads and had just taken a bite when she heard her phone ringing. "I'm sorry. I forgot to shut it off. I'll do that now."

"If the call's important, go ahead and take it."

She shook her head. What could be that important? She took the phone out of her purse, opened it to press the off button, saw the caller was Molly and stifled a sigh. Molly knew she was out with Simon. She hadn't been happy when Chloe told her, but even so, Chloe couldn't believe she was calling.

"Did you do any more packing today?" Simon asked when she turned her attention back to him.

"No. I was actually kind of lazy."

"Good. Everyone needs a lazy day."

They chatted a bit more until their salads came and then busied themselves with eating. Chloe was always hungry lately, and food this good deserved her attention.

The steaks were delicious, too. In fact, everything was, and Chloe enjoyed herself tremendously. Simon was a wonderful host, attentive and entertaining. He told her stories about his childhood and in turn, gently queried her about hers.

"It was hard when my mother left," Chloe admitted. "I was so young, and I didn't understand. I thought it was my fault." The memory of that time brought a familiar ache. "My dad was devastated, broken. He never recovered."

Simon's gaze never left hers, and in his eyes she saw not just sympathy but understanding. "Your aunt was there for you, though."

"Yes." Chloe smiled. "She's more like my mother than my own mother ever was." Chloe tried to keep the bitterness out of her voice and knew she was only partially successful.

For the remainder of their meal, he continued to ask questions about Chloe's growing-up years. She told him about her uncle and what a good man he had been, she told him about high school and college and he, in turn, told her about his school experiences and growing up as a Hopewell. He also talked about his father, and she could see that he'd admired his dad and had tried to make him proud.

The evening passed so quickly that Chloe was surprised when the waiter came to clear their table. She took the opportunity to excuse herself and headed to the ladies' room. After using the facilities and freshening her makeup, she decided to check her voice mail to see if Molly had left a message. She had.

Molly sounded frantic in her message. "Chloe," she said, "I know you're out with Simon and you've probably turned off your phone, but when you get this message, please call me. I'm at Riverton Hospital with Mom. She had a bad car accident tonight—some drunk ran a stop sign and hit her broadside—and they brought her here by ambulance. She's in surgery right now, and I'm not sure exactly how bad it is yet. I know the EMT said her left leg was smashed up pretty bad, and apparently there are internal injuries. I'm so scared, Chloe."

Chloe's eyes were tear-filled as she hurriedly called Molly back. At first she was afraid Molly wasn't going to answer because her phone rang several times, but finally her cousin said a breathless, "Hello?"

"Moll?"

"Oh, Chloe! Thank goodness you called. Where are you?"

"I'm still at the restaurant. We just finished eating, and I decided to check my messages. How's Aunt Jane? Is she okay?"

"She's in recovery right now. Dr. Hagen said she came through the surgery fine. They had to remove her spleen. But it was her leg that needed the most work. I'll explain everything when I see you. Oh, God, Chloe, I was so scared."

"I'll be there as soon as I can. Are you staying at the hospital tonight?"

"Yes."

"Okay. Where are you now?"

"I'm in the surgical waiting room. But if she gets moved to a room before you get here that's where we'll be. Just ask at the desk. They'll know."

When Chloe returned to the table, Simon took one look at her face and said, "What is it?"

Chloe explained.

"I'll get the check and pay it," he said. "Then I'll take you there. Unless you want to go home first?"

"No, I want to go to the hospital first."

It took them almost an hour to get there. Simon pulled up to the entrance to the hospital. "I'll park and find you," he said.

"You don't have to wait," she said. "I might be hours."

"On the other hand, you might want to go home and change, then come back."

"I know, but I can call a cab."

He just looked at her. "I would never let you do that."

No, Simon would never abandon her. Never allow her to find her way home alone. If she wanted him to, he would always be there for her.

"Besides," he added, "I'd like to see how your aunt is doing. Maybe I can be of help."

Chloe breathed a sigh of relief. She was grateful that Simon wanted to stay, even as she'd felt she had to tell him to go. She'd bet even Molly would be happy to have him there, for Simon was a man who commanded respect, whereas sometimes women were ignored. Chloe hated admitting that, but it was true.

She found Molly still in the surgical waiting area. The two women hugged hard, and Chloe could see that Molly had been crying. "But Aunt Jane's okay, isn't she?" Chloe asked.

Molly nodded and swallowed. "I just…oh, Chloe, she looked so white…and so small when they wheeled her away!" Molly's eyes swam with tears. "Sh-she's always been so *strong*."

"I know." Chloe put her arm around Molly's shoulders. She could feel how her cousin was trembling.

"The doctors told me that she'll have to be in a wheelchair and will need weeks of physical therapy. She won't be able to manage on her own, so we'll need to get full-time help at home. I don't know how we'll manage. I mean, our insurance will probably cover the therapy, but it's not going to cover someone coming to the house. And we sure can't afford it. If only I wasn't teaching summer school, but we're right in the middle of the term. I can't walk out on them, and there are three more weeks left."

Chloe didn't even stop to think. "That's not a problem. I'll come and stay. At least during the day."

"But…you're moving."

"I'll postpone the move. You'll be finished with school by the middle of July, right?"

"Yes."

"So…it's only about two more weeks."

"What about your townhouse? And the movers?"

"The movers aren't a problem, and I don't think the landlord has my unit rented out yet. But if he does, I'll figure something out." She squeezed Molly's shoulders. "Look, Aunt Jane was always there for me when I needed her. I *want* to do this for her."

"Here you are."

Chloe and Molly both looked up. Simon stood there smiling down at them. Chloe could feel Molly tense, and her eyes darted to Chloe's. "Simon said he'd come and wait with us in case I needed to go home and change clothes."

"How's your mother doing?" Simon asked Molly.

So Molly explained the situation, finishing with, "And Chloe said she'll postpone her move and stay to help until I'm finished with school."

Simon's eyes met Chloe's. He didn't say anything, but she knew he was pleased. It'll be okay, she assured herself. She would only be three months' pregnant when Molly finished the summer school session. She would barely be showing. Loose clothing would take care of any additional weight gain. No one would know. She could probably even stay until the end of July, if she wanted to—if her aunt and cousin needed her to.

Simon had removed his suit coat and tie and left them in the car. He sat down in the chair next to her. Chloe wished now she'd gone home to change because she felt a bit conspicuous in her dressy outfit and killer heels—which were now killing her—but she didn't want to leave until her aunt was settled into a room.

"Are you planning to stay the night?" she asked Molly.

"I think so. Unless they say I can't."

"I'll stay with you, then."

Molly gave her a grateful smile.

Luckily, they didn't have long to wait. About twenty minutes later, a doctor approached. He was in his fifties, Chloe guessed, stocky with unruly brown hair and bright blue eyes behind rimless glasses. His name tag read Dr. Jon Hagen. Before he'd even greeted Molly he looked at Simon and said, "Hey, Simon. Good to see you."

"Hello, Jon. Are you Jane Patterson's surgeon?"

"I am."

"Ms. Patterson is really worried about her mother. If I'd known you were her doctor, I would have assured her that she was getting the very best care available."

Dr. Hagen smiled and turned to Molly. "She is, and we're pleased with how her surgery turned out. She came through everything with flying colors, and she's awake now and doing well. You can stop worrying. In fact, we're getting ready to move her to her room."

"Is she having a private room?" Chloe asked.

"Insurance only covers a semiprivate one," Molly said.

"Give her a private room," Simon said. "I'll take care of it."

"I can't let you do that," Molly said.

"Please let me do this for you," Simon said.

Molly opened her mouth to protest, Chloe was sure, then she abruptly shut it. Chloe was glad. She wanted her aunt to be as comfortable as possible; plus it would be difficult for Molly to spend the night if Jane was sharing her room with someone else. Chloe looked at Simon and hoped her eyes conveyed her thanks. When he smiled and nodded, she knew he understood.

If only I'd met Simon first.

How different her life would be now. She and Simon would be married. This baby she was expecting would be theirs. It would be loved and its birth joyfully anticipated. Chloe wouldn't be alone, nor would she or Molly be worrying about anything to do with her aunt's care. Simon would take care of everything.

But she *hadn't* met Simon first.

And they *weren't* married.

He didn't even *know* about the baby she was carrying.

Part of her felt so desolate that she could have cried for hours. The other part of her was just thankful she had this much of Simon—that for now, at least, he was looking out for her and hers.

Once Dr. Hagen left, a nurse came out to tell them what room Jane would be taken to. "You can go on up, and we'll see you there," she said.

Thirty minutes later, a still-sleepy Jane was wheeled into a lovely private room on the fourth floor and, after kissing her hello and making sure Molly was okay and didn't need anything from home, Chloe asked Simon if he would take her home to change clothes.

"I'll be back soon," she promised Molly. "Now are you sure you don't need anything?"

"Just bring an extra nightie and toothbrush, okay?"

"Okay."

Simon said he'd go and get the car and meet her at the front entrance. Ten minutes later they were on their way to her townhouse.

"I can't thank you enough for arranging the private room for my aunt," Chloe said the moment they were alone.

"I was happy to do it, you know that."

"It means so much to my aunt and to Molly. But I— I don't know how I'll ever repay you."

A heartbeat later, he said softly, "Chloe, don't you know by now that I'd do anything in the world for you?"

His simple words caused a storm of emotion: joy mixed with regret, hope mixed with despair and, overriding all, the pride that this exceptional man cared so much for her. She turned away so he wouldn't see her tears. If only the clock could be turned back and she could live the past year over again.

But it couldn't.

The past was the past.

All Chloe could do now was pray that the future would be better.

Chapter Thirteen

"Tell me about the dinner," Molly said. "You looked great, by the way. I love that dress."

Chloe smiled. "Thanks." The two women were sitting down the hall from Jane's room. Jane had fallen asleep about ten minutes earlier, and they hadn't wanted to talk in her room in case they would wake her.

"Was it fun?" Molly's question was almost wistful.

Chloe looked at her cousin. Was Molly *envious?* It was the first time Chloe had ever thought so—at least when it came to Simon—and the thought startled her. She tried to remember if Molly had been to the Riverton Lodge anytime in recent memory and couldn't think of an instance. In fact, since her cousin had dated Lucas McKee, Chloe couldn't remember her going anywhere except with gal pals. Feeling a rush of compassion, she downplayed the evening, saying only, "It was very nice."

Molly nodded. "It was really nice of him to get a private room for Mom."

"It was, wasn't it?"

"I know why he did it, of course. He wanted to impress you."

"He doesn't need to impress me, Molly. I already know what kind of man he is."

Molly looked at her sharply. "Chloe, you're not thinking you can have any kind of future with him, are you?"

Chloe shook her head. "No. I know better."

"I wish…oh, darn it, anyway. As much as I don't want you to go to Syracuse, I wish you didn't have to stay here longer because of Mom. Maybe I can get them to hire someone to take my place for the rest of the term."

"Don't you do anything of the sort! I'm a big girl, Moll. I can handle things with Simon."

"You keep saying that."

"Well, I *can.*"

Molly's mouth tightened. Chloe knew her cousin didn't believe her. Heck, she wasn't sure she believed *herself.* But really, she had no choice, did she? She would *have* to handle things with Simon.

Thinking of the reason why this was so, she put her hands on her stomach. Would she change her situation if she could? If for some reason she *wasn't* pregnant and she was free to pursue a future with Simon, would she choose that?

But there was no answer to her question.

Because she wanted her baby.

And she also wanted Simon.

Simon and Todd had settled into an uneasy truce when they were together at the family home, but at the office it was a different story. Simon wasn't happy with Todd's performance. Ever since he and Meredith had come home from Fiji, Todd had been doing less than his best at work. Or maybe it *was* his best. Simon didn't know because Todd had never spent enough time with his nose to the grindstone to show Simon one way or another if he could be a valuable employee.

On Tuesday morning, when the report Todd should have had on Simon's desk by three o'clock on Monday still wasn't there, Simon called Todd's extension.

Rosalie, Todd's secretary, answered. "Um, I'm sorry, Simon, but Todd's not here. Can I take a message?"

"Where is he?"

"Um…"

"Has he been in yet this morning?"

"No," she said reluctantly.

"Have you heard from him?"

"Not yet."

"When you do," Simon said through gritted teeth, "tell him to call me immediately. And I do mean *immediately*."

"I will."

Simon slammed down the phone. Todd was pushing it. The trouble with pushing it, though, was the pusher needed to have the advantage. And in this instance, he didn't.

What was Simon going to do about Todd? He couldn't

have his brother slacking on the job. It set a bad example for everyone else, and it caused bad feelings. All the other department managers had to tow the line. Todd could not be an exception.

For the next hour Simon worked on the quarterly forecast and tried not to think about Todd. At one point, he remembered that he'd meant to order flowers for Jane Patterson today, so he took care of that. Finally, at nine-forty-five, Maggie buzzed him to say Todd was on the line.

"Where the hell are you?" Simon said.

"Well, good morning to you, too," Todd said.

"Morning was 8:00 a.m. when you were supposed to be at your desk."

"Sorry. Meredith and I had a late night with her parents, and I slept through the alarm."

"Are you in the office now?"

"I'm in my car. I'll be there in fifteen minutes."

"Come here to my office first."

"Yes, sir!" Todd's voice mocked Simon.

Simon disconnected the call. He'd save what he had to say for when he had Todd sitting across from him.

It was twenty minutes—Simon timed him—before Todd showed up. "Sit down," Simon said, indicating the chair placed in front of his desk.

"I hope you're not going to give me some kind of lecture," Todd said. "Especially seeing as I haven't even had my coffee yet."

"And whose fault is that?"

Todd shrugged.

Simon studied his younger brother. Todd's whole problem was he was too good-looking and too charming for his own good. Maybe if Larissa hadn't spoiled and indulged him so much he might have turned out fine, but she had and he hadn't. Yet she wasn't the one suffering the consequences. Simon was. And Meredith would be at some later date when Todd reverted to type. Simon was increasingly glad Chloe had escaped with only bruised feelings. That was a whole lot better than a miserable marriage. Because if Todd treated marriage with the same disregard to his job, it would be miserable indeed.

Simon sighed and picked up the phone. "Maggie, would you bring my brother some coffee, please?"

Once Todd had his coffee, Simon instructed Maggie to shut the door. "Now," Simon said, "we have to get a few things straight."

"What things?"

Simon wanted to smack the insolent look off Todd's face. He forced himself to keep his voice from showing how angry he was. "You will either buckle down and do the job you're getting paid to do, or you will be terminated."

"What?" Todd stared at him. "You wouldn't dare."

"I would dare. In fact, I'm warning you. You will be out of a job unless you straighten up. And immediately."

"Just because I was late a couple of times?"

"That's just one of the things you've done that's unacceptable. The big problem is you're ignoring your assignments. For instance, where the hell is the department report that was due yesterday?"

"I haven't finished it yet. But you'll have it in plenty of time for Thursday's meeting."

"It was due yesterday. Every other manager had their report done on time. You're the only one who didn't."

"Simon, for crying out loud, what's the big deal? Yesterday, today, tomorrow? You just need it for the Thursday meeting, and I said you'll have it by then."

"It's not your place to tell me when I need the report. It was due yesterday. I don't have it. End of story."

Todd jumped up, nearly splashing what was left of his coffee all over Simon's desk. "You're being a hard-nose just to show me who's boss. What's your problem, anyway?"

"My problem, as you put it, is that I am in charge of this company. I have hundreds of people on the payroll, people who are depending on me to do a good job so that our company will continue to prosper and make money and pay them to do *their* jobs so that they can take care of their families. Part of my job is making sure my employees, *of which you are one,* do the jobs they're supposed to be doing. But you, Todd, are not doing your job. And now, that's become *your* problem. Which you had better fix. Right. Away." Simon stood, too. He was angrier than he'd been in a long time, but he kept his voice low.

Todd glared at him. "Go to hell, Simon." He turned on his heel and stalked from the room. The door slammed behind him. Simon could just imagine what Maggie was thinking. Of course, knowing Maggie, she'd probably listened in on their entire conversation. Not that she'd ever admit it.

It took Simon a while to erase the confrontation from his mind and settle back into his workday routine. He ate lunch at his desk to make up for the time he'd lost in dealing with Todd and hoped he'd be able to leave on time tonight so he could stop by the hospital and see how Jane Patterson was doing before his Tuesday-night squash game with an old college buddy.

At two o'clock, Maggie said Larissa was on the line. That surprised Simon. His mother had been ignoring his existence ever since he'd told her he wasn't going to be at the reception honoring Todd and Meredith.

"I think we need to talk, Simon," his mother said by way of greeting him.

"Oh? What about?"

"I think you know."

Simon stifled a sigh. "Mother, if I knew I wouldn't be asking."

"If I must spell it out, we need to talk about your abominable treatment of your brother."

Simon cursed inwardly. "So Mama's little boy has already tattled, has he? Why does that not surprise me?"

"I don't understand you, Simon. Why do you dislike your brother so much?"

Simon closed his eyes and counted to ten. "I don't dislike Todd." But was that really true? "I dislike his behavior. And his obvious belief that he's entitled to something around here, whether he does his job or not."

"For your information, he *is* entitled to something. He's one of the *owners* of the company, Simon, even though you seem to have conveniently forgotten this."

Simon laughed wryly. "All he's entitled to is his share of the company's profits every six months, Mother. Nothing else. His salary is not a gift or an entitlement.

His salary is paid in return for him performing a job to my satisfaction. And currently, actually for a long while, that hasn't been happening. And, as I told him earlier, if he doesn't soon straighten up, he will no longer *have* a job here."

"I forbid you to fire him. Do you hear me? I forbid it!"

"With all due respect, Mother, you have no say in whether he keeps his job or not."

"I'm on the board of directors!"

"No one on the board can tell me who to hire or fire."

"I don't agree."

"Oh, I see. So if Mark DelVecchio, for instance, starts doing a lousy job as CFO, but one of the board members doesn't want him fired, I should keep him. Is that what you're saying?"

"No, of course not, but Mark is not a Hopewell."

"Oh, I see. If your name is Hopewell, you can slack off as much as you want, is that it?"

"You are deliberately twisting my words, Simon. You know there's a huge difference between Mark Del-Vecchio and Todd."

"Yes. Mark does his job superbly, and Todd barely deigns to show up."

For a long moment, silence trembled between them. When Larissa did speak, her voice was glacial. "I have only one thing left to say, Simon. Do not cross me on this."

Simon sat looking at the phone after she'd hung up. For two cents, he'd tell her and Todd and everyone else on the board of directors to take their job and shove it. He was sick of the job. And he was sick of his family. For once in his life, he wanted to do something that made him happy. Well, there *was* one thing he could do. He could take the rest of the day off.

Five minutes later, he pointed his Lexus in the direction of the hospital. If he was lucky, Chloe would be there. And at least then, the day would not be a total waste.

The most gorgeous bouquet of roses Chloe had ever seen was delivered to Jane's room at two-thirty. There were two dozen of them, all white, ringed with lacy fern and arranged in a beautiful dark blue glass vase. The card read simply, "Here's hoping your injury mends quickly. Simon Hopewell."

"Oh, they're lovely," Jane said, her dark eyes filled with pleasure. "Such a nice thing to do." She looked at Chloe. "I have a feeling I know exactly why he's so attentive."

Chloe knew her cheeks were a bit pink, and she hoped her aunt didn't notice. Jane had no idea Simon was paying the difference between what the insurance company would allow for a semiprivate room and the large, airy private room she now enjoyed. Chloe was sure Jane would have plenty to say about it if she *did* know.

"Molly tells me Simon took you out to dinner Sunday night," Jane said.

"Yes."

"I thought you had decided to avoid his company."

"I did, but…" Chloe sighed. "As I told Molly, Aunt Jane, it's hard to say no to Simon."

"He likes you."

Chloe thought about denying it, but what was the use. They both would know she was lying. "I know. And I…I like him, too."

Jane's expression was sympathetic. "I think you more than like him," she said softly.

Chloe didn't answer. Instead, she chewed on her bottom lip and avoided her aunt's eyes. "It's so hopeless," she finally said.

"Why is it so hopeless?"

"Oh, Aunt Jane. You know!"

"All I know is, Simon Hopewell seems like a very fine man. He's single. You're single. What's the problem?"

Chloe lowered her voice. "You know what the problem is. I'm carrying his brother's *baby.*"

"Yes, I know."

"Well, then…"

"You know my feelings about this, Chloe. I think you should come clean with both Todd *and* Simon."

Chloe felt like crying. "I can't, Aunt Jane. He…he would probably hate me if he knew, anyway."

"I doubt that. He's much too sensible to hate you for something that happened when you and Todd were engaged."

"Well, he certainly wouldn't want to have anything else to do with me if he knew."

"I doubt that, too."

Chloe shook her head. "I—I can't take the chance."

Her aunt didn't reply for a while. When she did, she shook her head sadly. "I think you're making a big mistake, sweetheart, but it's your life. I can't make you do what I think is right. You have to make those decisions yourself."

The words were barely out of her mouth when there was a light tap on the door, followed by Simon's entrance. It was obvious to Chloe that he'd come straight from work because he wore dark slacks and a dressy shirt. He was carrying a Barnes & Noble bag, which he held out to Jane with a smile. "I thought you might like some reading material."

"Simon," she said, "you already sent those gorgeous flowers." She pointed to the vase of roses, which were on a nearby chest of drawers.

"Flowers are easy. You just call up the florist and they do all the work. I wanted to pick out some books I thought you'd enjoy."

Jane, flushed with pleasure, opened the bag. She took out three hardcovers. From the titles, Chloe knew they were all on the bestseller list. "Thank you so much," Jane said. "I love to read."

"I figured you did." He looked at Chloe. "I was hoping I'd get to see you today."

Chloe didn't dare look at her aunt, especially after the conversation they'd just had. She just hoped she wasn't blushing. Those darned butterflies that seemed to follow Simon wherever he went were back, and once again, they'd settled in the vicinity of her stomach. "Well, here I am," she said inanely. *Stupid, stupid. Why can't I think of clever things to say?*

"Luckily for us," Jane said, "we're going to see a lot more of Chloe in the next month than we'd anticipated."

"Yes," Simon said. "She told me." He smiled at Chloe. "Was your landlord as agreeable as you thought he'd be?"

"He was actually thrilled that I'll be staying on a bit longer because he hasn't rented it yet."

"So it works out for everyone."

"Yes," Chloe said. "Well, except for poor Aunt Jane, who isn't thrilled she'll have to use a wheelchair or go through physical therapy for weeks on end."

"I'll be okay," Jane said. "I just hate that I'm disrupting everyone's life."

"It wasn't your fault you got broadsided," Chloe said. "Besides, it's no hardship for me to spend a couple more weeks with you. You know that." She didn't dare look at Simon because she was thinking that it was also no hardship that she'd be spending a couple more weeks with *him,* either. When she finally did look at him, there was an expression on his face that caused her heart to skid.

And in that moment she knew that no matter how she tried to deny it that she and Simon were past the point of no return.

He loved her.

She could see it in his eyes.

And she loved him.

And one of these days soon they would not be able to walk away from each other.

Right now, Chloe was no longer even sure she wanted to.

Chapter Fourteen

By noon on Friday, Chloe and Molly had brought Jane home and gotten her settled in.

"Let me see what there is for lunch," Molly said. Her principal had gotten a sub for her, and she had the day off. "I'll probably need to go to the supermarket this afternoon. We're really low on fresh fruits and vegetables. Milk, too."

Chloe went out to the kitchen with Molly, and they decided their best bet was to make toasted cheese sandwiches and canned tomato soup. They were still trying to determine if there was enough bread to feed all three of them or if perhaps Chloe should go pick up some Subway or something when the doorbell rang.

"I'll go," Chloe said. "It's probably another plant or

something." Jane's coworkers and friends had been sending gifts for days.

But it wasn't a plant. Instead a young man in a Giant Eagle shirt stood outside holding a big box of groceries. "Delivery for Jane Patterson." he said.

"Wow. Wonder who sent all this?" Chloe held the door open so he could bring the box inside. It was probably from Jane's office.

"I've got one more out in the truck," he said.

"Who sent this?" Molly asked when the kid set the box on the kitchen table.

Chloe shrugged. "I don't know."

"There's a card in the other box," the kid said.

Molly started pulling items out: a foil-wrapped ham, a whole cooked chicken, lettuce, tomatoes, apples, carrots, celery, an English cucumber, a bunch of grapes, a big carton of strawberries and a half gallon of pralines-and-cream ice cream.

"Oh, yum," Molly said. "I'd better get this ice cream in the freezer."

Chloe grabbed the card off the second box and ripped the envelope open. "I figured the cupboard would be bare. Enjoy. Simon Hopewell." Chloe was stunned. She almost didn't want to show the card to Molly because she knew exactly what her cousin would say.

But Molly just raised her eyebrows and said, "You know, I'm not surprised." She continued unpacking items from the second box, which contained mostly cheeses and crackers, a couple of loaves of crusty bread, fancy olives and other delicacies, as well as cans of nuts and dried fruit. There were also two bottles of wine— one red and one white.

By now Jane had wheeled herself into the kitchen. "Oh, my," she said. "Who sent all this? Simon?"

"How'd you know?" Chloe said.

Jane smiled. "It doesn't take a genius to figure it out, Chloe."

Later that afternoon, Simon called Jane. Chloe knew it was him because she could tell from the things Jane said. She kept expecting Jane to hand her the phone. Jane concluded the call without doing so but not before asking him to join them for dinner.

"That was Simon," Jane said, eyeing Chloe.

"Yes, I thought so."

"I asked him to join us for dinner. You don't mind, do you?"

Chloe kept her expression noncommittal. "Why should I mind?"

"I was afraid you might find his presence uncomfortable."

Chloe *would* be uncomfortable with him there, but she wasn't about to admit it.

He arrived at five-thirty. He must have gone home first because he was dressed casually, in well-worn, soft-looking jeans and a burgundy knit shirt. He smiled at Chloe. "Is it okay that I came?"

"Of course." Why was it that all he had to do was look at her in a certain way and she got a hollowed-out feeling in her stomach?

"We're having comfort-food tonight," Molly said. "Mostly thanks to you." She actually smiled at Simon.

Dinner turned out to be more fun than Chloe would have imagined. Simon possessed a rare ability to put people at ease, and he kept her aunt and cousin entertained and amused. Even Chloe managed to relax, although not completely. How could she when Simon was so near?

At eight o'clock, when Jane began to yawn, Chloe and Molly excused themselves and got Jane ready for bed. Chloe had expected Simon to leave; instead he cleaned up the kitchen and was waiting for them when they emerged from Jane's room.

"Call me if you need anything," he said to Chloe.

"Thanks, but I think we'll be fine."

"Thank you again for all the food and everything," Molly said.

"It was my pleasure." Again, his eyes met Chloe's.

She wished he'd just go. Every time she looked at him, she remembered the kiss they'd shared and wondered if he was remembering it, too. She cared too much for him, and she was afraid every glance, every word, would give her away. Before Jane's accident, Chloe had actually thought she didn't care if he knew how she felt about him, but that had been crazy. Of course, she cared. The only way she could ever leave Riverton without him continuing to try to stay in touch with her was if he thought *she* didn't care. How could she have ever believed otherwise?

After he'd gone, Molly said, "I think I was wrong about him."

"Oh?" Chloe's heart sank. If even Molly was going to start extolling Simon's virtues, what chance did Chloe have?

"Yeah, I do. He's a pretty good guy. You could do a lot worse."

"Aren't you forgetting something, Moll?"

"You mean the little matter of the baby?"

"Yes. That little matter."

"No, I'm not forgetting. I'm just beginning to think more along the lines of what Mom thinks. Why don't you just tell Simon about the baby? It might not make any difference to him at all."

Chloe sighed heavily. "I cannot have this conversation again. Trust me, Moll, I can't tell him. And if he knew, it *would* make a difference. Not to mention that his knowing would open another whole can of worms because of course, if *he* knew, it wouldn't be long before his mother knew. What if Larissa Hopewell decided to try to take the baby away from me? With her money and contacts, she might actually be able to do it. I can't take that chance."

Chloe left soon after. She spent a restless night and woke up with a feeling of dread in her stomach. Somehow she had to make it through the next two weeks without allowing herself to weaken. That meant staying as far away from Simon as possible. And when he *was* around, she'd make sure she kept him at an emotional distance. It wouldn't be easy. She knew that. But she could do it. She *had* to do it, no matter what it cost her.

Unfortunately, Simon seemed to have the opposite goal in mind. Even though he'd told Chloe to call him if they needed anything, he didn't wait to be summoned. Instead, he fell into the habit of stopping by Jane's house at some time every day.

On Saturday, he showed up in the afternoon and wanted to know if he could run any errands for them.

He stayed more than an hour. And even though Chloe kept herself busy in the kitchen, out of his sight, every cell in her body was on high alert until he finally left.

On Sunday he showed up in the morning with a box of warm crullers from Trina's Bakery. He stayed until nearly noon. This time Chloe couldn't avoid him completely because Jane invited him to have breakfast with them. Chloe wanted to scream. And yet, her traitorous heart couldn't stem the tide of joy that his presence always produced.

On Monday he dropped by after work and, when Jane happened to mention how much she enjoyed Japanese food, he insisted on picking up a couple of orders of teriyaki chicken and a half-dozen fancy sushi rolls. And, of course, he stayed to share the food with them.

Every single day he found a reason to visit. And every single day it became harder for Chloe to imagine what it was going to be like in Syracuse when she would no longer see him.

By the time the last two weeks of summer school were over, Chloe felt completely drained from trying to maintain the fiction that she and Simon were simply friends and nothing more.

"So this is your last day here?" he said that Friday. The question was casual, as if he'd just thought of it.

Chloe avoided his eyes. "Yes." She smiled over at Jane. "Molly will be taking over from now on, and Aunt Jane's doing so well, pretty soon she'll be out of that chair all the time."

"When's your move taking place?"

"The movers are coming Monday."

He nodded. "Everyone's going to miss you."

"And I'll miss everyone." In fact, Chloe could no longer stand thinking how much she would miss them all.

Later, as Simon was leaving, he said to Chloe, "Walk me out? There's something I wanted to talk to you about."

How could she refuse? "All right." *Please, God. Help me be strong. Just this one last time.*

When they were outside he said, "Would you let me take you to dinner tomorrow night?"

If he only knew how much she wanted to say yes. "I'm sorry, Simon, I can't. Jane and Molly have planned something for our last evening together."

"I understand. What about Sunday night, then?"

Chloe shook her head. "I don't think so. I-I'll have too many last-minute things to do. The movers are coming really early on Monday morning." Her heart felt like a trip hammer in her chest. Could he hear it? Did he know how much it was costing her to refuse him? She swallowed. She knew she was ridiculously close to tears.

His eyes were dark pools in the twilight. "So I guess this is goodbye, then."

"I guess so." She would be eternally grateful that her voice did not wobble.

He leaned over and brushed her cheek with his lips. "I'll miss you," he said softly.

Before she could gather her wits enough to reply, he turned and got into his car. A minute later, he was headed down the street. Chloe stared after the car. She couldn't believe he'd gone so quickly and that he'd said so little. Didn't he *care* that she was leaving in three days? He hadn't even *tried* to get her to change her mind.

Still stunned by his abrupt departure, she walked slowly back to the house.

"What's wrong?" her aunt asked.

Chloe mentally shook herself. "Nothing's wrong."

Jane frowned. "Are you sure? What did Simon say to you?"

"Really, Aunt Jane, nothing's wrong. I—I was just feeling sad for a moment. I'll miss him. I'll miss *all* of you."

Soon after, Chloe said her goodbyes. Molly helped her carry all her things to the car. The two hugged, and Molly said they'd expect her about six the following evening.

Chloe managed to hang on to her composure until she was out of sight of the house. Then, and only then, did she allow her tears to come.

Chloe arose early on Sunday morning. Once again, she'd had a restless night. Telling herself she would not think about Simon, she took a shower, had her breakfast and began to get ready for the movers.

She worked all day on last-minute packing—mostly the things she would take to Syracuse in her car.

About three o'clock that afternoon, she began to feel hungry and realized she hadn't had any lunch. Deciding she would scramble some eggs and use the last of the cheddar cheese in the fridge to mix in with them, she headed for the kitchen. She had just put the small nonstick frying pan on the stove when the front doorbell rang.

She frowned. Now what?

But even as she walked down the hall to the door, she knew. So it wasn't a surprise when she looked out the peephole and saw Simon. For long seconds, she imagined walking away. Not answering. He would know she was home, of course, but he would get the message.

She actually took a step backward. Her heart was pounding.

The doorbell rang again.

Simon.

The ache in her throat grew. She blinked back tears. "Please go away," she whispered.

The doorbell rang a third time.

"I know you're in there, Chloe."

Whimpering, knowing she was weak, knowing the last thing she should do was open the door, she opened it anyway.

Simon took one look at her face and walked inside. The next moment she was in his arms, and he was kissing her. She knew she should say no, even as she closed her eyes and pressed herself close. The kiss went on and on, a fusion of tongues and lips and heartbeats. It became two kisses, then three. He kissed her eyes, her nose, her throat. His hands dropped to her bottom, bringing her even closer. She could feel how much he wanted her. Her own desire raged.

All thoughts disappeared. There was only sensation and need as his hands slipped under her waistband and down, cupping her buttocks. His hands felt hot against her skin, and she moaned as her body turned to liquid fire.

They never made it to the bedroom.

If she'd been thinking straight, if she'd been thinking *at all,* she never would have allowed him to pull down her shorts, to remove her T-shirt, to unsnap her bra. She would have pushed him away when his mouth found first one breast, then the other. She never would have reached for the waistband of his pants or unbuttoned them and helped him take them off. She never would have gone into the living room with him, never would have taken the rest of her clothes off, never would have tumbled onto the sofa with him.

She cried out when he touched her with his fingers, gasped when he replaced fingers with tongue. Instead of stopping him, she pressed his head closer and arched herself to feel him more fully. And just when she thought she couldn't stand the excruciating tension another minute, he plunged into her.

As if they'd been lovers forever, she wrapped her legs around him and met him thrust for thrust. Her climax came fast, a shattering prism of sensation that made her feel she was falling off a high cliff and taking him with her. He shouted when his own climax quickly followed hers and his life force poured into her.

Stunned by the force of her emotions, she clung to him, wishing she could stay in the protective circle of his arms forever. Relishing the feelings of safety, of home, she closed her eyes and allowed her spent body to drift into sleep.

The sound of the phone startled her awake. Disentangling herself from Simon's arms, she sat up and looked around. Amidst their castoff clothing, which lay scattered across the floor, Samson sat looking at them. In his steady gaze, Chloe imagined she saw censure.

Dear heaven. What had she done?

None of what had happened today seemed real. Making love with Simon felt as if it had happened in a dream, in a fantasy.

She stared at Simon, who was still blissfully asleep. If only she could go back to sleep, pretend everything was still the way it had been before Simon had arrived. Unfortunately, the fantasy was over, and reason and reality had returned.

And now Chloe was appalled. She couldn't believe what she'd done. What had she been *thinking?* That was the problem. She *hadn't* been thinking. She hadn't been thinking at all!

Beginning to panic, she grabbed her clothes from the floor and, giving Simon one last regretful glance, she tiptoed from the room.

Racing upstairs and into her bedroom, she closed the door behind her. For just a moment, she leaned against it. Her mind tumbled crazily; her heart pounded in her chest. *What am I going to do? What am I going to do?*

And then she heard Simon's footsteps.

With shaking hands she knew it was cowardly, but she whirled around and turned the lock.

Simon was so stunned when he heard Chloe leave the room. It took him a few seconds to gather his wits…and then his clothes. He dressed hurriedly, not bothering with his shoes, then followed her up the stairs. When he reached the second floor landing, there were two open doors and one closed door. After checking, he saw that the two open doors led to Chloe's office and a bathroom. Both were empty.

Walking to the closed door, he knocked softly. "Chloe?"

No answer.

"Chloe?" he repeated.

"Please go, Simon," she said. Her voice sounded muffled, as if she were crying.

"I'm not going until we've had a chance to talk."

"I don't want to talk."

"Chloe," he said gently. "I know you're upset, but we *have* to talk."

There was no answer.

"Chloe," he said, louder now.

Still no answer.

He didn't know what to do. Should he go in, even though she didn't want to see him? Talk to him? He reached for the doorknob. It didn't budge. She'd locked the door. That, more than anything else, shocked him. Was she *afraid* of him? "Look, I'm not leaving until you open this door. We *have* to talk. We…can't pretend this didn't happen."

"Please go away."

Now he could hear her crying. "I mean it. I'll camp out right here on the floor outside your room until you open the door. You can't stay in there forever."

Long seconds passed, and Simon was afraid he'd have to make good on his threat. But finally the door opened.

Face set, eyes bleak, Chloe stared at him. "What happened between us was a mistake. Please don't make it worse. I asked you to leave, and I meant it. I don't want to see you again. If you're really the gentleman you say you are, you'll respect that and go."

"You can't mean that."

"I do mean it."

Simon felt desperate. Talking to her was like talking to a brick wall. All the emotion they'd shared had disappeared as if it had never been. "But why? I love you, Chloe. I know the situation is a bit awkward with what happened between you and Todd…and my mother, but we can weather that, can't we?"

Chloe shook her head. "No. It's impossible. It's totally impossible. Please, Simon. Please just go."

"Didn't you hear me? I *love* you. And I think you love me. I want you to marry me. I want us to spend our lives together."

Suddenly, dismaying him, Chloe began to laugh. But the laughter was mixed with tears, and she seemed almost hysterical. Simon was alarmed. Something was terribly wrong. Why was she acting like this? He reached for her, tried to take her into his arms, but she pushed him away, her eyes filled with something very much like fear.

"Listen to me, Simon," she said. Her voice trembled, but it was filled with a steely determination. "We have no future together. I told you. What happened was a mistake. Don't make it into something more than it was. It was just sex. That's all. Sex. I'm sorry if I misled you. I—I…don't love you, and I don't want to marry you. Nothing has changed. I'm leaving Riverton. I'll be gone tomorrow night. And in the meantime, I'd appreciate it if you would leave me alone. I don't want to see you again…*ever.*"

With one last defiant look, she shut the door again.

Simon stared at the closed door for a long moment.

Why was she acting like this? He couldn't understand it. It *hadn't* just been about sex. He knew she hadn't meant that. So why had she said it? He'd told her he loved her. Didn't she believe him? No, that couldn't be it. She *knew* he loved her. Hadn't he shown her he did in dozens of ways? And she loved him. He'd be willing to bet on it. Chloe simply wasn't the sort of person to make love with him unless she cared about him. *Especially* him.

No. She was acting like this because of Todd and Larissa. Because of what his family had done to her. Said about her. Who cared what they thought? They weren't important. Why couldn't she see that despite his family the two of them could still build a good life together?

The silence of the house pulsed around him as he stood there trying to decide whether to stay and keep trying to make her see reason…or to go. Frustrated and feeling more impotent than he'd ever felt in his life, he finally made his decision and turned, walked downstairs and let himself out.

Chapter Fifteen

The move to Syracuse went off without a hitch. The movers came on time Monday morning, loaded up the truck quickly and efficiently and were gone by noon. Once the van moved off down the street, Chloe finished loading her car, then she cleaned out the fridge—which belonged to her landlord—and took out the last of the trash. The final chore remaining was putting Samson into the cat carrier, something he hated and Chloe dreaded.

But if Samson were making the trip with her, it had to be done. She accomplished the task by tempting him with some tuna, which he loved, then dropping a towel over him and wrapping him up so he wouldn't scratch her with his back claws.

"Sorry, old buddy, but this is for your own good," she said as she dumped him inside and closed the carrier.

He gave her a look that said he couldn't believe she'd betrayed him like this and emphasized his displeasure with a loud hiss.

"You couldn't be more miserable than me," she said.

Leaving the townhouse unlocked and the keys on the kitchen counter—she had a cleaning service coming in an hour—she put the last of her belongings in the car and pointed it in the direction of the freeway. Tears swam in her eyes, and sadness filled her heart as she drove slowly away from Riverton and everyone she loved.

"Twins? You're *sure?*" Chloe stared at her new ob-gyn.

Dr. Sandoval smiled. "I'm positive. Look. You can see two heads and several legs. Because one of the babies is hidden behind the other, I can only tell the sex of the one in front. Do you want to know?"

Chloe grinned. "Yes, I do."

"It's a girl."

A girl! She would have a daughter. Maybe two daughters. Or a daughter and a son. No matter what, Chloe didn't care. Just as long as both babies were healthy. Her expression must have conveyed what she was feeling because the doctor smiled again—this time reassuringly.

"Everything I can see indicates they're fine. And since you're past the first trimester, you should be out of the danger zone. We'll keep close watch, of course, and you must take really good care of yourself, but everything looks great, and I think you should have two healthy babies."

Chloe left the doctor's office with a chaotic mix of emotions. She was ecstatic, frightened, sad, awed and thrilled—all at the same time.

And yet…overriding all the wonderful feelings was the underlying fear. The thought of *two* babies instead of one was daunting. It would have been hard enough to raise one child alone. But two? And without any help or support?

Chloe bit her lip. She would manage. She *had* to manage. Because she had no other option.

Simon couldn't settle down to anything—not work, not golf, not squash, nothing. All he could think about was Chloe. Day in and day out, she monopolized his time and his thoughts. He tried to forget about her. He told himself if she didn't want him then he didn't want her, either. He wasn't going to beg.

But he could not get her out of his mind.

A month went by.

Then two.

It was mid-September now, and the leaves on the maple trees were beginning to turn. Autumn had always been his favorite season. In the mornings, there was a little nip in the air, promising cooler weather. Fruit and vegetable stands popped up on all the country roads. There'd been a bumper crop of corn this year, and everyone was selling it, promising theirs was the tenderest and sweetest to be had. Soon, pumpkins would be for sale, too, along with apple cider and apple butter.

This year, none of it appealed to Simon.

Chloe…and only Chloe…was important.

She had changed the number of her cell phone, but he easily found an online service to uncover the new number. Then, ashamed he had bought such information, he resisted the urge to call her. Clearly, she didn't want him calling. Besides, he didn't want to talk to her. He wanted to *see* her.

He wished he had someone he could confide in. Maybe get a different perspective and some advice. Unfortunately, his so-called friends were mostly business associates or guys he played golf and squash with. The most personal discussion any of them had ever had was about the last presidential election or who might win the Super Bowl. The only person he could think of as a possible confidante was Jane Patterson.

The more he thought about talking to Jane, the more he gravitated toward the idea. So the third week of September, in desperation, he rang Jane and asked if he could take her out to dinner.

"Why, that sounds lovely, Simon. I'd love to go."

He took her to the Riverton Lodge. He could see by the pleasure in her eyes that it was a good choice. Realizing she probably didn't get many opportunities to dine somewhere like the Lodge, he felt bad that he'd never thought to invite her there before.

He waited until they'd finished their entrées and had their coffee and dessert before introducing the subject of Chloe.

"I wondered when you'd get around to asking about her," Jane said. Her eyes were kind as they studied him over the rim of her coffee cup.

"Please tell me what to do," Simon said. "I can't let her go."

"Have you called her?"

He shook his head. "No. She told me she didn't want to hear from me ever again." He grimaced. "Actually, she said she didn't want to *see* me again. But I still feel like driving to Syracuse and sitting on her doorstep until she comes outside, then carrying her off whether she likes it or not."

Jane smiled. "Like the cavemen used to."

"Sometimes being a Neanderthal helps. At least that's what they tell me."

"Every woman's fantasy…" Jane mused. "Being carried off by the big, strong man."

"*Is* it every woman's fantasy?"

Jane ate a bite of her crème brûlée. Her reply was thoughtful. "I don't know. It was never *my* fantasy, but every woman is different. I do know one thing, though. If you truly love Chloe, I don't think you should give up."

He could see in her eyes that she wanted to tell him more. *What?* he wanted to say. *What?* "I know you feel you have to abide by whatever you promised Chloe. Just tell me one thing, though."

"And what is that?"

"Does Chloe love me?"

Jane looked at him for a long, tense moment. Then she nodded. "I believe she does."

That was all Simon needed to know. He didn't ask Jane to reveal Chloe's address. He could find out where she was living easily enough. All he did was smile and say, "Thank you."

Later, as he walked Jane to her door and said good-night, she hugged him briefly, then said, "Good luck. I'm pulling for you." She took her keys out of her purse. "Oh, and Simon?"

"Yes?"

"Chloe's birthday is Wednesday."

For the first time since Chloe moved away, Simon's heart felt light. He whistled all the way home.

Chloe planned to take Wednesday off. She worked doubly hard Monday and Tuesday so that she could. She figured a girl's thirtieth birthday should be treated as a special day, so she'd booked a manicure and pedicure, as well as a haircut in the morning, and in the afternoon she intended to shop for baby clothes, as well as a couple of maternity outfits because she had grown out of everything. In the past month alone, she'd gained seven pounds. The mound that was her stomach looked as if she had a basketball inside. It was actually kind of alarming because she still had three and a half months to go. But Dr. Sandoval said she was right on schedule for weight gain with twins.

"You'll lose it quickly once those babies are born," she'd added with a smile.

Wednesday dawned clear and bright, a perfect late-September day. The weatherman had promised a high of sixty-two, but the morning air was chilly. Chloe decided she would dress in layers and was just putting the finishing touches on her makeup when her doorbell rang. She glanced at her watch. A few minutes after nine. Who could that be? But even before getting to the front door, she realized it was probably a birthday delivery from Aunt Jane and Molly.

So she was smiling as she opened the door. Sure enough, a young man stood there holding a vase of gorgeous fall flowers. And just as she'd guessed, the accompanying card read, "With all our love on your thirtieth birthday! Jane and Molly."

Fingering the diamond heart pendant her aunt and cousin had given her as a going-away gift, Chloe realized once more that even though her life wasn't perfect she had more than a lot of people have. She had Jane and Molly, two of the most thoughtful and loving women in the world. And she would soon have two beautiful babies. She resolutely kept her thoughts away from what she didn't have.

Who she didn't have.

After making sure Samson had clean litter and enough food and water to keep him happy, she set out for the salon and a morning of pampering herself.

That afternoon, she spent several pleasant hours buying baby clothes and a few more maternity outfits. Her one extravagance, a completely indulgent purchase that she knew she should pass up but couldn't, was a spectacular red lace dress that she could wear for Christmas. Where she would wear it, she didn't have a clue. She only knew she couldn't resist it.

"It would look gorgeous on you," the sales clerk said. "Try it on."

Even her baby bump looked pretty in the dress, and Chloe couldn't stop smiling as she pirouetted in front of the three-sided mirror.

"Some sparkly red sandals would be perfect with it," the helpful clerk said. "I saw the perfect pair downstairs."

So of course Chloe had to buy the shoes, too. And while she was at it, she bought silvery earrings and bangle bracelets to match.

What was it about spending money on beautiful clothes that made a woman feel so good? Thoroughly happy with herself, Chloe drove home with a song in her heart. For some reason, today everything seemed more hopeful. More positive.

The moment she turned the corner onto her street she saw the Lexus parked across from her unit. She didn't even have to look at the license plate to know whose it was.

Her heart leaped into her throat, and her pulse went crazy.

Dear God.

She didn't know what to do. What should she do? Should she turn around and drive off? But where would she go? And, anyway, she couldn't stay away forever. Besides, knowing Simon, he would sit there waiting for her until she finally was forced to come home.

Oh, God. He'll see that I'm pregnant.

Maybe she could just stay in the car. If she put one of her bags on top of her, maybe he wouldn't notice that her stomach came up almost to the steering wheel.

You're being ridiculous, Chloe. Face it. The game is up. Just pull into the driveway and park your car. Then get out and get this over with.

Two minutes later, taking a deep breath for courage, Chloe opened her car door and got out. She stood by the car and waited. She didn't have to wait long.

Simon, too, got out of his car. As he walked toward her, she could see the stunned expression on his face. She took another deep breath and girded herself for what was to come.

"Chloe?" he said as he came closer. His gaze dropped to her very pregnant stomach.

She could see the wheels turning in his head. Knowing him, she guessed that at first he might have imagined the baby to be his. After all, they hadn't used any protection that fateful night when they'd made love. But also knowing him and how intelligent he was, she knew he would very quickly put two and two together.

"Would you help me get these packages inside?" she said, walking over and opening the trunk of her car. "We can talk there."

Wordlessly, he took all the packages except one small one and followed her up and onto the porch. She quickly opened the front door, and they walked inside.

"Where do you want me to put these?" he asked.

"Just dump them on the dining room table," she said, pointing to the small dining room on the right.

Then she led the way into the living room where she immediately sat in the rocking chair. "My feet hurt," she said, kicking off her clogs. "I've been out all day."

"Yes, I know. I've been here since eleven this morning." He smiled crookedly. "Happy birthday."

"Thank you."

They looked at each other for a few seconds, then he nodded and sank down onto the sofa. "This is why you said the two of us were impossible."

"Yes."

"The baby's Todd's?"

"Yes."

She could see that he was experiencing a jumble of emotions, but he didn't seem to be angry. Instead, he seemed thoughtful, as if he were adding everything up in his head and coming to terms with it. She was grateful for that. She didn't think she could handle a big, emotional, angry scene just now. She felt too drained. Too tired. And too sad.

He finally spoke. "I wish you could have trusted me enough to tell me."

"I didn't want Todd to know. Or your mother." This last statement was said defiantly.

He nodded. "I figured that out."

"I *still* don't want them to know." Chloe was close to tears now, but she would fight them with all her strength. The last thing she wanted was Simon's pity. *Just get this over with.*

Simon sat forward. "Chloe, your pregnancy doesn't change anything as far as I'm concerned. It makes no difference to me. None at all."

Chloe stared at him. Her heart was pounding so hard it scared her.

"I love you," he said. He stood, then walked over to her. Reaching for her hands, he pulled her up and put his arms around her. "I love you," he said again. "I want to marry you. I want to take care of you and your baby. It'll be *our* baby. I'll love it just as if it *had* been mine. Don't you know that?"

Chloe heard him, but she wasn't sure she believed him. How could he say this? Didn't it matter to him that she was carrying his brother's children? That his mother couldn't stand her? That she'd lied to him?

"We don't have to live in Riverton," he said. "We don't ever have to see my family if you don't want to. I'll do whatever it takes to make you happy, whatever it takes to make you feel safe. All I care about is you. I care more about you than anything else in the world. Don't you know that by now?"

Looking into his eyes, Chloe saw the truth of what he was saying. He *did* care more about her than anything else. Her eyes filled with the tears she'd been fighting. "Does...does that apply to two children?" she asked.

"Two children?"

"Yes." She smiled through her tears. "I-I'm having twins."

She knew she would never forget his smile. Or his words. "Chloe, my love, if you were having a *dozen* babies, I would still feel the same way."

And then he kissed her.

The kiss was a bit awkward because her belly got in the way, but they managed. And in that kiss, which was filled with passion and tenderness and love and promise, Chloe knew that she had finally found where she belonged.

Epilogue

Anna leaned over to whisper in Chloe's ear. "Poor Larissa. It must kill her to have to smile and pretend to be happy."

Chloe grinned at her sister-in-law. She and Anna were sitting together on the love seat in the music room. Simon and Noah stood talking at the bar while Todd stood alone, his back to the room, staring out the window. A storm had blown in from Canada the day before, and the grounds glistened with snow under the bright afternoon sun. Larissa, as always, sat in her favorite chair, a large whiskey and soda clutched in one hand. Max lay at her feet.

It was the first time today that Chloe had been able to relax because the twins, Julie and Jane, were down for their afternoon nap upstairs in the old nursery. The twins were now twenty-two months old, and they were a handful. And in five more months, they'd be joined by a baby brother. Chloe wasn't certain she could handle three children under three, but she guessed she'd have to. Of course, Simon kept telling her she could have a nanny or any other help she wanted, but she felt it was her place to raise her children, not some stranger's. She smiled, remembering how he'd rolled his eyes and muttered about how stubborn she was.

"What do you suppose is going on with Todd and Meredith?" Anna asked softly. "I still can't believe she stayed home and let him come to Riverton alone."

Chloe shook her head. "Simon thinks they're having problems."

"Serious problems?"

"It sounds that way."

"Poor Meredith."

"I know. I feel kind of sorry for her, too." Chloe couldn't believe she was saying this, but she actually meant it. It couldn't have been easy for Meredith when Chloe and Simon married. Especially since Simon had persuaded Chloe that there was no reason they couldn't live nearby. They didn't actually live in Riverton; instead they'd built a home halfway between Riverton and Mohawk. It was far enough away from Larissa yet close enough to Jane and Molly…and now Anna, who had become one of Chloe's dearest friends. She gave

Anna a fond smile and thought how beautiful her sister-in-law looked in her russet taffeta maternity dress. Anna's baby—also a boy, according to her ultrasound—was due in March. Noah was beside himself with excitement and pride. It was sweet to watch.

Maybe that's why Todd seems so unhappy. Because both Noah and Simon will soon be fathers. Yet Todd knew he was *already* a father. It saddened Chloe that he seemed so disinterested in the twins, even though it thrilled her that Simon acted as if they were his. No father could be more loving or attentive.

She glanced over at him. She loved him so much. She would be eternally grateful that he hadn't paid any attention to her objections to their relationship and had come to Syracuse to find her.

All her worrying had been for nothing. Oh, things weren't perfect with Simon's family—except for Noah and Anna, of course—but they weren't nearly as bad as Chloe had feared. It helped that Todd and Meredith had moved to Manhattan within six months of Chloe and Simon's wedding and that they didn't attend a lot of family functions, but even if they hadn't moved away, Chloe knew she would have been able to handle the unusual situation.

The reason was Simon. Unlike Todd, he never permitted his mother to say one unkind or critical remark to or about Chloe. He stood up to Larissa and let her know that if she didn't treat his wife with respect and courtesy, he would resign his position with the company and he and Chloe and their children would move away. Far away. It wasn't an empty threat and Larissa knew it. So from the first, even though she was far from happy about their marriage, she had behaved herself.

In turn, Chloe was always courteous and respectful to *her*.

I'm so happy, she thought. I never thought I'd ever be so happy.

As if he knew she was thinking of him, Simon's gaze met hers. And in the long look they exchanged, Chloe knew he felt exactly the way she did. Heart full almost to bursting, she decided she was the luckiest woman in the entire world.

* * * * *

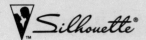
Silhouette®

COMING NEXT MONTH

Available June 29, 2010

SPECIAL EDITION

#2053 McFARLANE'S PERFECT BRIDE
Christine Rimmer
Montana Mavericks: Thunder Canyon Cowboys

#2054 WELCOME HOME, COWBOY
Karen Templeton
Wed in the West

#2055 ACCIDENTAL FATHER
Nancy Robards Thompson

#2056 THE BABY SURPRISE
Brenda Harlen
Brides & Babies

#2057 THE DOCTOR'S UNDOING
Gina Wilkins
Doctors in Training

#2058 THE BOSS'S PROPOSAL
Kristin Hardy
The McBains of Grace Harbor

SSECNM0610

REQUEST YOUR FREE BOOKS!

2 FREE NOVELS PLUS 2 FREE GIFTS!

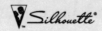

SPECIAL EDITION
Life, Love and Family!

HARLEQUIN®

A Romance

FOR EVERY MOOD™

Spotlight on
Heart & Home

Heartwarming romances
where love can happen
right when you least expect it.

See the next page to enjoy a sneak peek
from Silhouette Special Edition®,
a Heart and Home series.

Introducing McFARLANE'S PERFECT BRIDE
by USA TODAY *bestselling author Christine Rimmer,*
from Silhouette Special Edition®.

Entranced. Captivated. Enchanted.

Connor sat across the table from Tori Jones and couldn't help thinking that those words exactly described what effect the small-town schoolteacher had on him. He might as well stop trying to tell himself he wasn't interested. He was powerfully drawn to her.

Clearly, he should have dated more when he was younger.

There had been a couple of other women since Jennifer had walked out on him. But he had never been entranced. Or captivated. Or enchanted.

Until now.

He wanted her—*her,* Tori Jones, in particular. Not just someone suitably attractive and well-bred, as Jennifer had been. Not just someone sophisticated, sexually exciting and discreet, which pretty much described the two women he'd dated after his marriage crashed and burned.

It came to him that he...he *liked* this woman. And that was new to him. He liked her quick wit, her wisdom and her big heart. He liked the passion in her voice when she talked about things she believed in.

He liked *her.* And suddenly it mattered all out of proportion that she might like him, too.

Was he losing it? He couldn't help but wonder. Was he cracking under the strain—of the soured economy, the McFarlane House setbacks, his divorce, the scary changes in his son? Of the changes he'd decided he needed to make in his life and himself?

Strangely, right then, on his first date with Tori Jones, he didn't care if he just might be going over the edge. He was having a great time—having *fun,* of all things—and he didn't want it to end.

Is Connor finally able to admit his feelings to Tori,
and are they reciprocated?
Find out in McFARLANE'S PERFECT BRIDE
by USA TODAY bestselling author Christine Rimmer.
Available July 2010,
only from Silhouette Special Edition®.

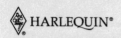
HARLEQUIN®

Showcase

LESLIE KELLY
Naturally Naughty

Wicked & Willing

On sale June 8

Reader favorites from the most talented voices in romance

Save $1.00 on the purchase of 1 or more Harlequin® Showcase books.

SAVE $1.00 on the purchase of 1 or more Harlequin® Showcase books.

Coupon expires November 30, 2010. Redeemable at participating retail outlets.
Limit one coupon per customer. Valid in the U.S.A. and Canada only.

52609057

5 65373 00076 2 (8100)0 11654